Infernal Infinity

John P. Warren

CONTENTS

Title Page

Copyright

CHAPTER ONE   1

CHAPTER TWO   8

CHAPTER THREE   13

CHAPTER FOUR   19

CHAPTER FIVE   22

CHAPTER SIX   25

CHAPTER SEVEN   28

CHAPTER EIGHT   32

CHAPTER NINE   36

CHAPTER TEN   45

CHAPTER ELEVEN   49

CHAPTER TWELVE   56

CHAPTER THIRTEEN   67

CHAPTER FOURTEEN   79

CHAPTER FIFTEEN   86

CHAPTER SIXTEEN   90

CHAPTER SEVENTEEN   95

CHAPTER EIGHTEEN   105

CHAPTER NINETEEN   111

CHAPTER TWENTY   115

CHAPTER TWENTY ONE   118

CHAPTER TWENTY TWO   126

CHAPTER TWENTY THREE   134

CHAPTER TWENTY FOUR   140

CHAPTER TWENTY FIVE   145

CHAPTER TWENTY SIX   153

CHAPTER ONE

Across from the glowing spatial reefs of ice and rock that beckoned against the distant still thunderous asteroid belt that beckoned the ailing Earth. A world now devoid of life and where the remaining two hundred and fifty thousand plus survivors of humanity now lived on the lunar biosphere called Apollo City.

A man is not truly living unless he has a conflict to give it a rightful purpose, twenty-four year old Jim Callaghan thought as he watched the bereft Earth from the window. He had enough conflict to go around, enough to give his life meaning beyond his normal life span and many times over. He imagined a time before he was born when the asteroid belt went seemingly awry and bombarded the Earth, causing cataclysmic planet-wide destruction and how the fortunate were left on the artificial biosphere on the Moon escaping this calamity. How beautifully the rocks must have glowed in the dusky sky on a warm July night and how they gave no warning or subtle harbingers, just a 'goodbye mankind' to all down on Earth. So ruthless, so absolute. Not much different to the present day where Governor Edmund Sears applied the same principles in governance throughout the biosphere. He thought even hate can be just as powerful a motivator to give purpose to one's life, if not even more potent than love or simple desires or ambitions and this hate combined with a fervent anger at being denied any chance that this young man had of bettering himself and the would be advantages of the fruits of his labor such as love and sex. The means to simply better oneself were nonexistent and only available to the privileged and not the broader community on Apollo City.

Jim, a slim, good looking young man with an old head on his shoulders, was extremely jaded with the lack of opportunities in his sector – the poorest sector – of Apollo City.

"You know that's becoming contagious," a voice said, disturbing Jim's reverie.

"I don't get you, Richard."

"Day dreaming, of course."

"Oh."

"Jim, you can't afford to be helpless even for a moment if you want to overthrow the Sears regime."

"Just thinking how all this happened in the first place, the asteroid bombardment forty odd years ago. I'm trying to recall the name of Apollo City's chief designer but can't remember it."

"Not surprising. Sears hasn't given you young people much of an education. His name was Thomas Jenkins. He reportedly died a few years after Sears took control. Now I came to tell you that I've got five more people interested in joining."

"What good is an Underground if we don't have objectives that will lead to action and wipe out Sears and his motley crew?"

"Come on, Jim. If anybody can get him in the end, it's you."

"I don't want to kill anyone. We will be just techno-terrorists, knocking out municipal systems, being thorns in Sears's side. If we hurt anybody we will become the monsters and I don't want blood on my hands. This biosphere has its inauguration in violence – there's gotta be a better way."

"I understand but we have the right to self defend."

"Of course."

"Now are you ready to perform that speech?"

"Ready as I'll ever be."

Richard Barker was a lot older than Jim. He had known his parents and kept an eye out for him. Jim was preparing to give a speech encouraging new members to join his Underground in one of the poorer, disadvantaged sectors of Apollo City, Sector 954, his home.

He arrived at the almost derelict housing blocks and moved over to what he called "Concrete Square" because of its insipid appearance compared to the affluent Crystal Central which was located in the center of the biosphere and was where the rich had access to everything that Sears promised in a so-called Utopian society for all. All, that was, except the ones who sustained Sears's society, like Jim and his now deceased parents before him and everyone else in the poorer outlying sectors.

He stood up on a makeshift podium made of marble and was about to say the first lines of his speech when he felt dizzy and a surge of cerebral energy flooded his brain. Images of mathematical equations filled his conscious mind. He was about to verbalize them when he noticed a small crowd gathering waiting for him to speak so he quickly reasserted himself and regained his composure.

"We must stand together as one against this

unjust, brutal regime that has governed for so long. Until there is a fair distribution of wealth and the biosphere's top medical and scientific resources and services madeavailable to all, I ask you to join this revolt against the Sears autocracy. Join us!"

A standing ovation was given to Jim as Richard guided him to a nearby safe house. Jim turned to Richard and said in a serious manner, "At least if we fail, we can always go back to this very moment and try again."

Richard was gobsmacked at what the newly inaugurated leader of the Underground just said. "What do you mean?"

"I'd better lie down. I have such a headache coming on."

"Maybe that's not a bad idea, Jim."

Jim went inside to a small room where there was a soft bench for him to lie. He was supine and his head became flooded with ideas, realizations of time, space and causality. He tried to slow these thoughts down in order to process them but as he experienced moment after moment of clarity he deduced something that he could never believe to be true and uttered to a confused Richard Barker, "Richard, I think that I have finally cracked the mystery of everything. However, I can't give it credence."

"Get some rest, Jim. You're beginning to scare me."

"Don't you see? We have lived in this time line an infinite number of times before and will do infinitely again. Each time is exactly the same – the cycle of causality repeating itself until time and space ends then the exact same cycle beginning over again. When we die, the next thing we each remember is the moment that we are born again so we can live our lives the exact same way as before, no difference. What we do and think, we have repeated it over and over!"

"If that were true, Jim, we would remember our past lives, other cycles of causality that occurred before this one."

"You see, Richard. You only remember once. It's impossible to remember other cycles of causality."

"But you just said moments before all of this babbling if we fail, 'we can try again'?"

"Only if it has happened before."

"I'm afraid you're not making any sense."

"All we do, all that happens is predestined and there's nothing we can do about it."

"Okay, Jim. Say you're right, you can tell me if we will succeed against Sears or not."

"I don't know but I think I'm remembering something – scientific knowledge – that I haven't even studied yet."

Richard sighed to himself. He found himself wondering if Jim was the right man for the job as leader of the Underground.

"So, you're saying we don't have a chance against them because it sure as hell sounds to me like you're having second thoughts on taking on the regime."

"That's not what I meant."

"Did you ever hear the old saying 'if you conceive it, you can make it happen?' You have decided we have failed already."

"Believe me, Richard – I intend to win!"

Suddenly there was a loud explosion near the barrier that separated each of the poorer sectors of Apollo City that interrupted their philosophical quandary. Sears had these barriers erected because of his paranoid fears of giving any chance of camaraderie forming amongst the more disgruntled of the biosphere's residents.

"That's not one of ours?" Jim asked Richard.

"No, it came from inside Sector 953. Sears is on to us!"

"Let's keep a steady head, Richard. We have to get out of plain sight right now."

Two members of Jim's resistance went over to casually investigate the explosion. To their amazement, three citizens came out from the smoke. One young woman and two middle-aged men.

"We are here to meet Jim Callaghan and Richard Barker!" the young woman said.

They were brought to a safe house before being checked out fully. Jim was staring at this beautiful young woman and thought how pretty she was. It was a moment of instant mutual attraction that he had been waiting his whole life for. He turned to her. "I'm open to ideas you may have on making the widest impact on the regime, Sophie?"

"That's right. Sophie Ramirez. There is a parade in Crystal Central the day after tomorrow. We can plant explosives to disable the municipal police--"

"No, that sounds much too reckless. If we set off explosives we could end up maiming or killing innocent people. We will have a peaceful protest and try to surreptitiously gain as much information on the biosphere's AI controlled infrastructure as possible because whoever controls the mainframe controls the biosphere."

Sophie didn't care too much for that response but

was being drawn to Jim's morals and personality as well as his looks. "Okay, Jim Callaghan, we will do it your way. I have gathered almost eighty people that will join the Underground if you'll have them."

Richard nodded to Jim.

"Certainly, the more the merrier. I will have my people work the finer details with yours and together we will give the Sears regime a message to notice our contempt toward the government of Apollo City."

A man and a woman no older than Jim joined Sophie's people. They sat down and got ready to discuss the logistics of the Underground's objectives on the parade, which was marking four decades of Sears' rule. This would be a daring message that had underlying goals of bringing down the biosphere.

CHAPTER TWO

A security laser beam pierced the crowd as they paraded placards containing slogans: "Thank You Governor Sears for Forty Great Years," "Long Live Governor Sears" etc. These people didn't really care - about a third of the population were subservient and their role was to provide for the rest of these privileged citizens their essentials and luxuries. The laser beam was capable of checking the citizens' DNA profiles to see who should be parading in the exclusive but restricted centralized area of Apollo City called Crystal Central. The poorer citizens like Jim, Richard and Sophie, as well as their families, were demanded to carry out all the essential work to sustain the biosphere, thus allowing for Sears and his chosen 'good stock' to live in his own type of secluded Utopian type society. Across Crystal Central were glass models of tigers and elephants as well as of various birds. These monuments were constructed around the time the biosphere was completed.

Richard Barker had his prized invention yet marauding high up above Crystal Central – a drone – capable of surveying the best exit for a group of Underground supporters led by Jim to protest peacefully at the injustice of society on Apollo City. As the tiny drone - which was about half a meter in length - scanned the vicinity, it almost crashed into the biosphere's glass transparent dome. This shield was designed as a multi-phasic defense mechanism to deter rocks and radiation from space. He quickly regained control by remote and continued his scans of the center of the biosphere, an area with the scent of opulence.

Back in Sector 953, Jim and Sophie were leading a group of fifty protesters, each carrying their own placards displaying slogans such as: "Fair distribution of wealth for all on Apollo City," and "Equality for assured mutual benefit for all," etc. They had hollowed out tunnels under the Moon's surface using laser technology designed by none other than Richard Barker. They entered these tunnels with lighting attached to their jumpsuits. Jim and Sophie followed the crowd in. Jim was feeling a combination of excitement and determination, hoping to impale the cold exterior of the Sears propaganda machine by letting these privileged citizens know the rest of the population's plight. It would take them over an hour to reach Crystal Central but they moved steadfast to that destination.

They were now located minutes from Crystal Central. Jim tapped on the button to activate the comm link to Richard who had sent the telemetry from his drone. Two of the Underground picked up laser rifles and cut upward through a thin layer of rock. They cut through the surface of a vacant area of Crystal Central's surface to allow them inside. It took twenty eight minutes and they had put on oxygen masks to breathe and protect themselves from the dust. As soon as there was a clear entrance, two other members who were carrying a ladder erected it upright and Jim followed Sophie after she climbed up it. They came out in a quiet corner of Crystal Central and could hear the pomp and razzmatazz of the celebrations.

"Disgusting, isn't it?" remarked Sophie.

"That it is," replied Jim, as he signaled the others to follow suit.

The remaining Underground members rushed out of the tunnel and lined up. Some were carrying the placards. Jim instructed them to charge into the crowd and shout about the injustice they were subjected to. He knew they were safe because the last thing Sears would do was to have them hurt. After all, they were the most able bodied men and women who had to do all the dirty jobs to sustain the elite's lavish lifestyles. He also figured the security would be unarmed because they would never see this protest coming.

Jim led the group of protesters through the crowd who were celebrating their dishonest good fortunes. They yelled, "Fair distribution of wealth and equal rights for all."

Then out of nowhere armed municipal police assaulted the protesters, taking them by surprise. They shot dead most of them. Jim and Sophie ran while Jim gestured to as many of his people to follow him. However, some were so consumed by rage that they fought hard, grabbing rifles off the municipal guards and firing at them, even killing some of them. There was pandemonium. Jim knew it was a losing battle and grabbed Sophie, who was about to pick up a rifle, and pulled back inside the tunnel. The protest hadn't gone according to plan. In fact, it was a disaster.

Jim was angry. Rage surged through his stomach to his heart. He screamed. Sophie hugged Jim to console him. They quickly sealed the entrance located in Sector 953.

Two days later and there was a widespread feeling of despondency among the residents of the poor sectors of the biosphere. Richard approached Jim and Sophie. They were busy trying to explain to the victims' loved ones why their cause was worthy enough to be sacrificed for.

"Jim, they will understand in time. We must continue the fight," Richard said.

"They must have had prior knowledge of our protest. We have a traitor."

"The AI controlled mainframe would have calculated all possible scenarios for the regime. That's how they beat us."

"How do we fight artificial intelligence? We don't stand a chance. Is it really worth dying for? We may not have luxury but at least we have some safety, even if it is from a brutal regime. I can't continue as leader of the Underground. I made an unsound calculation and got many killed. I'm just not cut out to be a freedom fighter."

Richard turned to Sophie. "Could you excuse us, love, just for a moment?"

"Sure," replied Sophie as she went over to the corner.

"Jim, you can't quit now. They may have AI but you have precognition. You must use those precognitive skills you keep telling me about – use science to beat Sears – the AI Interface."

"Some gift. I couldn't even foresee the massacre."

"Stop feeling sorry for yourself! Let me emphasize it to you, whoever controls the AI controls the mainframe."

"If we attain complete control over the mainframe – we control Apollo City."

"That's right, Jim. We need you as leader of the Underground now more than ever."

Sophie, who was busy staring at the biosphere wide news feed, alerted Jim and Richard to pay attention. She increased the volume. It was Sears himself addressing Apollo City.

"Residents and to the good residents, I vow to safeguard you from terrorists. Not only will there be increased security and checks but in addition to these, I am reintroducing neuro-resequencing treatments. The proletariat have too much imagination. Artistic expression fuels their imagination, leading them to think in terms of rebellion. Art, literature and science is for the privileged only. At least they can consume it in a civilized manner."

Sophie's skin almost turned to pure white. "I received those treatments as a child – they're barbaric! They're trying to turn us into vegetables!"

"That bastard!" cried Jim.

"Science, Jim. That's the weapon needed to fix Sears."

CHAPTER THREE

It was now three months after the Underground's failed revolt against the Sears regime. In Sector 954, the secret door way between neighboring Sector 953 had been well concealed by Jim and Richard.

"What are you up to?" asked Sophie Ramirez to Jim, he had always been something of a technophile. Jim turned to quantum science which he was illegally studying as a form of personal protest and because he was a dilettante in the field he quickly developed a taste for it and combined with the precognitive glimpses of knowledge he was surely on to something. He considered himself the exception to every rule in life and his veins were like rivers of despair over the helpless lives of his people.

"It is simply fantastic, and it could change our lives for the better from day one. I have to get it working properly first though. I'll tell you about it in time," answered Jim, with growing enthusiasm. "I am the person that's going to change the world... or Apollo City at least."

Sophie was eager to find out what kind of project Jim had been working on. She always believed what Jim said was true and perhaps even profound in some way. Even though she was close to Jim, she desired him to see much more in her than just a pretty face. They were both looking out the window at space.

"It's beautiful, isn't it?" asked Sophie.

"Look at Old Earth. It's so alone and desolate. It's hard to imagine it being filled with life, people, animals, trees and flowers and massive cities," said Jim, who was feeling nostalgic for a place he and Sophie had never laid eyes on.

"It gets pretty lonely here. What I wouldn't give to have one day on Earth," said Sophie.

"If you were on Earth today, you would either freeze to death or choke to death," Jim said, not altogether sardonically.

Sophie's current assignment for the Underground was to give the impression she wanted to seduce Sears's personal assistant Sam Crawford.

"You know what to say if he asks where your loyalties lie?" Jim asked her.

"I know well what to say," answered Sophie, feeling a little angry. "It's important we get to make this statement effectively."

"I don't know, Sophie – somebody or people might die, and I don't want that on my conscience."

"Jim, it's important that we do this. 'For far too long the ruling class and their followers had everything with their devices that do just about everything for them. Are we better off?

They have untold comforts while people we care about live in squalor and we break our backbones to oblige their luxurious lives just because they were lucky enough to be born in the right section of society. There is an unfair distribution of wealth throughout this biosphere. Our people have nothing while they have everything and all in the name of repopulating Old Earth to create even more elitist societies.'"

"I suppose a few carefully planned explosions won't hurt anyone, I guess, and famous words by the way."

"Glad you recognize them since you first said them to me rehearsing your speech as the founder of the Underground until Sears clamped us down," Sophie replied with a smile. "Anyway, it's what I believe too, Jim. There should be no destitute in our society especially when the administration claims to be affluent in every way. You think someone would realize that society on Apollo City would be more productive and happier if they shared the wealth with all the citizens."

"I agree, Sophie."

Crawford was Sears's right-hand man. He had an eye for pretty girls and an even more trained eye for the Underground. Sophie prepared for her assignment and deep down Jim was confident she could pull it off successfully.

Sophie was having supper at home in her apartment. It was evening by Earth's Greenwich Mean Time, which Apollo City had adopted as its standard time. "That spicy chicken sandwich was too spicy for me. I think I'll eat some fruit in the evening supper from now on." She had decided to go to bed early. She went into her room and opened a compartment where a canvass was concealed well enough with blankets. She took it out and picked up brushes and oils hidden underneath it.

"If only," she said to herself, sighing with helplessness at the mental block she had to her gift because of the neuro-resequencing treatments she received as a child and had managed to dodge their re-introduction.

She was a born artist. She began to scribble a circle on the canvass; it could be the moon. She looked at the selection of oils to find a suitable color and chose gray, a color that she thought was appropriate. It represented the stagnant area of her mind which once poured with very colorful, creative juices.

"Will I ever paint again? Was I ever truly an artist?" She was finished sketching. She wrapped a blanket around the canvass and hid it away. Sophie had a great zest for life as a young girl. She was in tune with her artistic side, which made her feel whole. Because it had been brutally taken from her, her reasons for continuing were minimal. "I almost wish I was never alive. No, I wish I was on Old Earth studying art at one of their European universities. I'd see all the greats' works, and I could do my damn best to emulate them.

People from all over the globe would come to see them. I could have been hired to do portraits of distinguished people or of everything I could find inspiration. How wonderful it would be..."

She was nearly in tears. She laid on her bed and began to stare at a blank white ceiling. "How wonderful it would be..." she said to herself and was more and more determined to see Sears's government pulled down, even more so than Jim. She headed back to Sector 953 where her mother had evening supper prepared for them including her ill father. As she entered their self-contained family apartment her head was miles away because she was indeed in love. She tapped the security code on the console to let herself inside her family home. Her mother had evening supper ready and waiting. It was just a simple protein dish. Her mother gestured to her to sit and eat. Sophie had built up an enormous appetite trying to avoid neuro-resequencing treatments as well as her as maintaining her duties for the Underground. She ate her meal quickly much to the notice of her mother whom was becoming increasingly uneasy. "Sophie, I hope you gave what I told you some thought? Your father is not getting any better. The sooner you are married to someone from the more affluent sectors the better."

Sophie did not want to hear that. She was besotted with Jim and anyone else would cause her uneasiness and great unhappiness deep inside her soul. "I know, Mom. I'm keeping a watchful eye out for the right man."

"You are so young and beautiful. I just don't want you to end up with some loser from the poorer sectors, that's all especially since your father's life depends on a partnership with the right man from the right background."

"I will do you proud, Mom."

CHAPTER FOUR

The other members of the Underground were now growing to respect Jim. He had their complete confidence. The Underground's seemingly simple objective was manipulating the mainframe computer, which was responsible for the entire city's day-to-day operations, and using it to gain control of Apollo City. Whoever controlled the mainframe controlled every piece of equipment on the biosphere because it regulated the biosphere's central AI network.

Jim had now reached a difficult, risky decision in ordering Sophie to plant a device that would cripple the mainframe and turn over control of it to him.

Sears was now aware of the Underground's presence and was taking drastic measures to wipe its known one hundred and eighteen members out. Since the failed revolt they got sympathy and some support and Jim recruited the little people from Sears's government and obtained information about the infrastructure of the city's inner chain of command, which endeavored to portray a squeaky clean image.

The Underground was not militaristic in its organizational structure; Jim Callaghan ran it more like a science field study team. They would not hunt down their perpetrators but rather arrest them. They would kill in self-defense though. So far their success had been minimal. Jim believed in hitting Sears with one major blow that would wipe them all out altogether. He didn't believe in just causing a little mischief here and there. The government's heavily guarded quarters was the target. Also, there was a sophisticated security system that was almost impossible to penetrate and hack into using unconventional means. So the Underground needed to successfully compromise the mainframe computer and replace it with their program to effectively gain control. With this achieved, they planned to arrest Sears and his colleagues. Then a trial and citywide election would be held to place Jim Callaghan in charge formally.

Jim was as much attracted to Sophie as she was to him. They had known each other for some time but because of his social disadvantage, he found himself in a position where he could not sustain any kind of relationship with her. Unknown to him and deep within himself this frustration fueled his need to rebel.

He was becoming a highly respected as a leader. There were some in the Underground who thought he was too much of a pacifist, and that a hardliner approach was required to remove Sears. This led him to begin a more hardline approach. He was not a killer unless, as with the Underground's ethos, it was self-defense. He had one chance, and if he failed, radical elements in the Underground would surely oust him as the leader, and God only knew who would replace him. He was aware of this. He knew he couldn't afford to fail.

Sophie had just finished her coffee when she turned to Jim and said she'd better be off. "Are you feeling a little nervous about your first job for us?" Jim asked.

"Just a little," she answered.

She stood up and brought her cup to the sink where she washed it out. "Could we meet up later?"

"Sure. How about Restaurant Apollo around four?"

"Four's fine."

"Catch you later then," she said as she headed out the door and smiled back at him.

Jim took the last drink from his cup and began to ponder.

"How great Sophie looked this morning. We make a great team. She's so different from the other women on this rock. They all think my head's up with the stars. When this is all over, I'm going to ask her if we could be more than friends, a partnership," he said quietly to himself.

CHAPTER FIVE

Sophie was sitting down at Restaurant Apollo, waiting for Jim for their informal date. The restaurant was Governor Sears's idea of keeping the working class happy. The other opulent bars were strictly for the upper-class. Restaurant Apollo was like its name – insipid and sterile as it could get for a venue designed for social interaction and fraternization among the biosphere's poorer citizens. Sears didn't have much imagination. He had strict, cold logic.

"There's a wedding on today," Jim said to Sophie with a smile.

"I'm sure they'll make a great partnership," Sophie replied with a little hostility.

"I know what you're thinking, Sophie. You used Sears's word partnership. Whatever happened to romance, like on Old Earth?"

"I don't know. Damn! Why did it have to happen … this city, the asteroids and why a bastard like Sears?" Sophie said, even more hostile.

"We'll get rid of him, Sophie, and trash out his values and place new, improved lifestyles for everybody on this city, the way it was on Earth," assured Jim.

"Damn right we will, and I'm gonna start with Sears's pet Crawford!" Sophie said asserting herself.

"I think we should iron it out one last time," demanded Jim.

"I know the routine short of sleeping with him, Jim. I'll say I find him very attractive, and I hope he thinks I'll make a good partner. Sorry … wife. You know what I mean."

`   "Don't make it too obvious."

"I won't. I can be subtle."

Sears and Crawford had heard rumors about the possible existence of an Underground; however, they hadn't really paid much credence to it. Sophie placed her hand on Jim's and smiled. "Don't worry, Jim. I'll pull it off!" she said tenderly.

Jim's expression appeared to bear reassurance. Jim then took out a small device and showed it to Sophie.

"What's that?" asked Sophie.

"It's a type of transceiver that will short circuit the mainframe's AI circuitry. I didn't tell you about it earlier just in case there are possible security risks. It's something Richard Barker invented. It will give me access to Crawford's user level account. Hey, I'm starving. What's on the menu?"

"The usual durum and soy-based delectable

dishes."

"It's not like we have much choice."

"Is there a chance there could be an explosion, Jim?"

"I'd be lying if I said that there was a minimal chance, but I know you will do this right. The last thing I want is for anyone to get hurt."

"I want to do this. I'll be very careful."

They left Restaurant Apollo and made their way to Sophie's apartment, where they saw posters of Sears being placed on the walls by two guards. "That monster!" Sophie said, nearly livid.

They entered the elevators and began to kiss passionately. When the doors opened, they composed themselves as the other residents walked to their own apartments along the corridors. They moved towards Sophie's quarters. A few moments later they arrived and entered them. As she moved closer to Jim, they resumed their kissing.

"I wanted to be with you completely after I complete my assignment. Then it will be right."

"I want the same, Sophie. I always wanted to be with a woman like you.".

"Really? I'll bet you did!" said Sophie in a playfully sarcastic tone.

Jim smiled. "No, it's not like that. I think we're kindred spirits. That's all."

"You know, Jim Callaghan, I think you're right," Sophie responded as she gave Jim a warm embrace.

CHAPTER SIX

"Richard!" Jim Callaghan yelled.

"I'm over here, Jim. I'm finished. Sophie shouldn't have much trouble planting that little surprise in Crawford's home," Richard Barker assured him.

"I sure hope she can pull this off, Barker."

"She can, Jim," Richard answered simply but effectively to Jim's increasing anxiety on Sophie's first assignment.

Richard Barker had invented components for Jim's explosive device and other ingenious pieces of technology which had taken Richard months. A lot of the time Jim didn't even tell him what their use was.

Richard was next in line to Jim Callaghan in the Underground's chain of command. It had been a not so typical week for Richard – enduring the highs and lows of progress and frustration of his work and also making sure the device operated within the safe ranges. It was also one week away from the anniversary of Abigail Barker's death. Sears's government personnel had effectively murdered her. She died of a massive stroke caused by an overload during one of her neuro-resequencing treatments.

Abigail had the gift of a singer and songwriter. Richard fell in love with her because he was captivated by her mellifluous tones the first moment he had the rare pleasure of hearing her sing. She was afraid to be heard singing because she dreaded the treatments so much, which she said gave her headaches. They had both joined the Underground two years before and were acquainted but never serious. At first, they were congenial to one another but developed strong feelings for each other over time. Richard had dealt with the loss of his wife by devoting himself to his work. One could say that Jim Callaghan was the scientist and dreamer who came up with the most "out there" ideas, and it was Richard Barker, the inventor, who put Callaghan's dreams into practical technology... technology with one purpose – to overthrow the Sears administration.

Richard had not quite gotten over the loss of Abigail. Although he believed he would meet her again someday, he was not sure how or where this would happen. He hadn't told anyone because the last thing he wanted was for everyone in the Underground to think he had lost it completely. Just before Abigail had lost her life, they planned on starting a family. This was obviously a difficult blow for Richard to take; however, he still was adept at his work for the

Underground.

Jim inspected Richard's device. "This is really something. Are you sure it will work?" he asked.

"Of course it will work. I haven't let you down yet," Richard responded vigorously. There was a quiet pause for a few seconds.

Jim looked at Richard and said softly, "It's coming up to Abigail's anniversary, isn't it?"

"Next week, Jim," Richard answered. Anger now filled his otherwise subdued visage.

"We have to get that bastard Sears!" Richard demanded.

"We will... all of them" assured Jim.

"She had the most beautiful voice I've ever heard, and she wrote a song especially for me. Just as she was singing it to me, those guards came and took her away. All she was doing was using the gift that God gave her," Richard said.

Richard was missing Abigail so much and was looking so sad, which filled Jim with even more contempt for Sears than he could have thought.

"I promise you, Richard, Sears will pay for her life," Jim said once again assuring Richard. He believed Jim. Together they could do it.

CHAPTER SEVEN

"**D**on't tell me it's the damned Underground again! And I use the term Underground euphemistically," Governor Sears exclaimed to Sam Crawford, his right-hand man.

"I'm telling you we must take them seriously, sir," warned Crawford.

"The security on my city is airtight, Sam; however, find out who's involved and bring their names to me," requested Sears.

"Yes, sir," answered Crawford.

Governor Sears was in his mid-sixties. He had been in charge of Apollo City for over forty years. Being a historian and computer technician who had worked his way up the ranks of the Apollo City administration, Sears found Earth's history to be intriguing and took all aspects of past human civilization and its varied fates very seriously. In his first five years as governor, he published and enforced his views on how life and society should be on the biosphere. He wanted to create "a more evolved civilization" which would one day repopulate Earth when it became habitable again. He quickly built up a following because he was one of those people that had the power of persuasion. He could tell you there were two kinds of rocks on the moon, and you would believe him.

Sears began to stare intently at Crawford. "Sam, I've chosen you as my successor. You will be the one to take my place when I pass on," he said.

"I'm honored, sir," Crawford responded humbly.

"You might have the job much sooner if the Underground blows my head off," laughed Sears.

"I'm sure that won't happen, sir," assured Crawford.

"Our measures will be more than effective to wipe them out completely. They're just fools trying to be bandits of some kind. What are the opinions of ordinary citizens on our policies?" asked Sears.

"You still have a loyal following, but a tiny minority are becoming brainwashed by those bandits," answered Crawford.

"We'll have to remedy that, won't we?" Sears asked.

Crawford nodded his head.

The pressure was brewing from the pit of his stomach. Sears became more serious and had something important to say to Crawford - not a favor to request but an order to give. "Sam, it has come to my attention that you're living your life licentiously, if not precariously," he said to

Crawford in a concerned manner.

"I am sorry if I have offended you, sir. I have a weakness for beautiful women," Crawford answered as if he were begging for his life, or more to the point – his job.

"Sam, your lifestyle to date is debauchery and upsets order aboard this biosphere, not to mention the bad example it's portraying to the general population and the administration. I can't afford this. I'm telling you as a friend to have one woman and establish a partnership. I have no children of my own. You can start a family and have an heir. You're the closest to a son I have. I'm ordering you to do this, or it will be your head that's blown off, and you replaced in the administration," said Sears threateningly.

"Yes, sir. I'll carry out your orders as always." Sears was pleased with Crawford's response.

"We begin the transition no later than today," said Sears.

"Today, sir? Crawford asked, taken aback.
"I am giving you higher user level access to the mainframe, Sam," elaborated Sears.

"That's great, sir," said Crawford.
This new level of access would increase Crawford's knowledge of the biosphere and the knowledge only Sears was privy to.
Sears could cause the biosphere's computer systems to shut down or completely self-destruct the biosphere in the event of a coup. That was the reason no one had ever dared to

challenge him. He also had a device planted in his right arm that could only be used by him, which in turn gave him remote access to the mainframe to initiate station self-destruction.

CHAPTER EIGHT

A middle-aged, overweight man extinguished his cigarette as his young girlfriend handed him some gum. They were part of an audience in a smoky nightclub. An attractive woman performing on stage was singing a beautiful ballad, which had captivated the entire audience as if they were under some siren spell. She finished the song with the final lyrics saying, "I know your love is true and transcends all time and space." Suddenly Richard Barker woke up. He was experiencing a profuse cold sweat and said to himself gently, "Abigail!" He got up and found a glass and poured himself some cold water. He was feeling a little dazed.

"How could it be? It was her! It was Abigail!" He took a drink, quickly followed by two more. "Where was that place? What was it? There's nothing like that on Apollo City," he said feeling a little confused on what he had dreamt.

Richard used finding inspiration in his dreams for his latest inventions. This kind of dream was an aberration, or could it had been a premonition? He pondered on this for a while and came to the conclusion that it was some destiny thing; perhaps he was to meet Abigail sometime shortly. The venue in the dream was nowhere on the biosphere. He thought maybe a victory was imminent; maybe instead it was a message.

Richard stared at Abigail's picture and began to imagine what their children would have looked like if they had had any. He was brimming with emotions of happiness, but he soon came back down to the painful reality that this would never be, and his emotions turned to anger. He went into his bathroom and made preparations for a shower and shave, which was a chore he found mundane. Richard would rather spend the twenty-four hours in each day wholly devoted to working on his inventions. He was now working on the final stages of a mechanism to relay signals for Jim Callaghan's quantum computing experiment.

After his shower and shave, Richard got dressed. He put on his wrist phone and entered Jim Callaghan's identification code.

"Good morning, Jim," he said.

"Richard. It'll be an even better morning if you tell me you're nearly finished," Jim said.

"I'm on the last stages, Jim. I have to say I've never done anything this complex before. I had to make a lot of improvisations. I don't think you'll have any problems," answered Richard.

"Problems! What kind of problems?" asked Jim

with deep concern.

"Relax, Jim! It will all go smoothly," answered Richard.

Jim always took on Richard's assurance that all should go well with the equipment. He knew Richard was the best in his field. Richard used to work for the Sears administration until he got fired because he did not report Abigail's practice of songwriting. It was not so much the singing that was outlawed as what the songs were. Abigail used to have references in her songs about the administration, particularly focusing on the lack of emphasis on romance and suitability when people were being instructed on how to choose a partner. Sears was not romantic. He believed that both people embarking on a prospective partnership should choose each other because they work well together and would instill this kind of efficiency in their children. The main reason Abigail's music angered the authorities was a particular song with a homosexuality theme, which was outlawed by Sears.

In some cases, the neuro-resequencing treatments were used on gay or bisexual men and women to change their orientation. This angered Abigail. She believed this kind of treatment was utterly barbaric and became one of her main motivations to join her husband in the Underground. Richard found her strong sense of values very admirable. The function of the equipment he was putting together for Jim eluded him. Jim did not tell Richard what he was going to use it for and the surprise motivated him even more.

Richard entered his workroom and adjusted the electromagnetic damping field, which prevented detection of his equipment and tools by the authorities if they decided to scan his apartment. He had been lucky not to come under direct suspicion because his record had been impeccable. The authorities never really questioned his loyalty. They believed Abigail was the bad apple of the relationship. Richard began to connect all the pieces. He didn't keep notes or records on his work. His memory was his backup and the only hard copy. He was now almost finished with the first stage of his work.

"Something's wrong. This won't connect to this without causing some cascade reaction. Jim would be furious," he said.

He continued working on it for a few more minutes. "Not much good," he muttered.

There was a problem. The equipment didn't seem to be working out the way it should. He had to begin again and redesign one of the gadgets.

"Great! Just when I thought I had all nearly completed. Well, there goes my lunch break," he said as he began determinedly to study it further.

CHAPTER NINE

Sam Crawford was sitting at a table for two in Restaurant Apollo. He was wondering to himself if Sophie Ramirez would even show up. What he thought was a date actually was her first assignment. He was pettish in waiting for her to join him. The assuagement of his misery was here; she arrived dressed demurely wearing an attractive garment.

"Sophie, welcome," Crawford said.

"Hi, Sam. Sorry, I'm late," Sophie said very apologetically.

"It's fine. I'll wait for you any time," he said awkwardly.

"I'll bet you would," replied Sophie.

She smiled, but she was frowning inside. "So what do you do in the administration?" she asked.

"Well, I make sure everything runs smoothly for all the residents," answered Crawford pompously.

"And you sure do excel in that regard. All the residents are upstanding citizens. Their offspring will be prime specimens to repopulate the Earth, and there will be social harmony and a crimeless utopian paradise," Sophie said with slight sarcasm.

"That's our great governor's plan," Crawford responded.

"Sam, I'm wondering if we could be a little risqué?" asked Sophie.

"How risqué?" asked Crawford.

"We could be a little naughty. You could have the chef do us up a decadent dish, something from Old Earth."

She took Crawford by surprise. He always strove to live for the moment, so he carried out Sophie's request.

"I'll be back in a few minutes," he said as he headed over to the kitchen.

Sophie pressed a button on a communications device, which also acted as a watch. Everybody in the city had one. It could be used to call people up just like a telephone. She placed it near her mouth and whispered, "Jim…"

"Sophie… status?" asked Jim in a reduced volume.

"It's going great so far. I think he is really into me," responded Sophie.

"Don't spend too long with him. You could let something slip accidentally," said Jim.

"I know what I'm doing. Remember to call me in an hour. Talking to him makes my skin crawl."

"Jim out," he concluded. Crawford returned to the table.

"I think you will be very pleasantly surprised at what I ordered for us," he said confidently.

"What is it?" asked Sophie.

"I'm not good at describing things. The chef will prepare it and bring it to us soon. I must say he was reluctant. He thought it was a ruse or some test, but I managed to convince him otherwise," bragged Crawford.

"I hope you didn't twist the poor man's arm," asked Sophie.

"Of course not. I'm a diplomat, after all," answered Crawford.

Crawford became more serious in his tone. "I have a modest status on Apollo City, and I think it's time I settled down and formed a partnership. My wife-to-be would have the same status bestowed on her," he said.

"Is this some proposal?" asked Sophie. Crawford laughed.

"Would you be interested if it were?" he asked.

"I could be tempted. After all, you possess the powers of persuasion," answered Sophie.

"Excuse me, sir, madam!" said the chef. "I decided to present to you one of my favorite dishes," he continued.

"I certainly hope you don't prepare this dish regularly?" asked Crawford.

The chef nearly turned white.

"Of course not!" he said apologetically.

"That's good to know," remarked Crawford.

"What is it?" asked Sophie.

The chef was about to answer when Crawford interrupted him. "I don't think we should say what it is publicly."

The other diners at Restaurant Apollo pretended not to notice what was going on. The chef returned to the kitchen. Sophie and Crawford began eating.

"Hmm, it is exquisite!" Sophie said.

"It's something you could get used to," said Crawford.

Sophie simpered and decided to change the subject.

"What do you think of Governor Sears's policy on artistic suppression?" she asked abruptly.

"I support it one hundred percent," responded Crawford.

"Why? What is so wrong about a natural talent like painting scenes such as the moonscape with Earth overlooking it in the distant background?" she continued.

"Nothing. Absolutely nothing to tell you the truth. It's when the artist begins to make certain statements in his work that creates the problem," answered Crawford.

Sophie suddenly was not enjoying her meal while Crawford was ravaging it as if it were one of his favorite dishes.

"Governor Sears has studied Old Earth's history and its various cultures. He knows where they all went wrong. We are a part of humanity's future where law and order are everywhere,"

Crawford elaborated.

"You know the best way to learn if I would be a suitable candidate for your wife would be to take me home. I hope you don't think I am too forward," Sophie said, trying to speed proceedings up.

This was not a quality Crawford was looking for in a prospective wife, but he was very attracted to Sophie. Not many men throughout the biosphere would refuse her.

"Let's go!" Crawford said without wasting another second.

As they got up and left, Crawford ordered the waiter to dispose of their meals quickly.

"I can't wait to see your residence," Sophie said holding his hand. She was slightly nervous hoping that Jim would make the call to her at the right time. The thought of making love to Crawford turned her stomach over. They took Crawford's private chauffeur-driven tram, which all the members of the administration had.

"I could become accustomed to this," Sophie said as she enjoyed the rare piece of luxury she seldom got to experience.

"This could all be yours, Sophie," Crawford said, trying to sell himself and his privileged lifestyle to her further.

"A girl has to wait and see, Sam. You wouldn't want someone that jumps the gun, would you?" asked Sophie.

"I like a woman that knows what she wants

and who knows her mind," answered Crawford.

They arrived at his residence, a typical self-contained apartment block. It reeked of opulence compared to the conditions in which Sophie grew up. Each one of these apartment blocks could hold fifty families. There were hundreds set out towards the outer rims of the biosphere.

Crawford's apartment block housed most of the administration's officials and their families. A garden surrounded each of these apartment blocks. Gardens were rare except for the public garden and park located in the center of the Apollo City biosphere.

"Allow me to show you my humble residence," said Crawford.

"I'll try to be flattered," said Sophie. She hated every second she had to spend there. She felt like ripping his heart out. Crawford was partly responsible for her neuro-resequencing treatments. She hated him as much as she hated them.

"I'll just freshen up and be with you in a few moments," Crawford said as he walked over to his bathroom.

Sophie was not one bit surprised that he put himself before her instead of asking her if she would like to freshen up first. This was her opportunity, though, and she knew she was running out of time. She looked around and located his remote access computer and placed the transceiver underneath the unit where Jim instructed her. She was not sure if that was the right spot, but she trusted her strong gut feeling. The doors of Crawford's bathroom opened.

"What are you doing over there?" Crawford yelled.

"Sorry! I'm just admiring your lovely home. And I'm seeing how the other half lives," answered Sophie nervously.

"You're going to be part of that other half – the better half," said Crawford.

Sophie was nearly sick after hearing that but kept her composure. Crawford began kissing her. She wanted to resist but knew that this was part of the job. In a way she was preparing herself for a life with another man, a life without Jim so she could save her father and please her domineering mother. Self sacrifice came easy to her even if it meant unhappiness. When she couldn't be an artist, everything took second place because only being able to paint made her truly happy. She had a feeling that Jim would understand in the long run because both of them were like sailors on a fragile ship in turbulent waters and storms would erupt along their journey of life – a life of denial of the means to express oneself in society.

"I want to freshen up," Crawford said. "You make yourself comfortable here – I won't be too long."

He went to the shower room while Sophie glanced at the mainframe's user terminal. She quickly took out the tiny explosive device and planted it behind the user terminal's screen. It stuck magnetically to the metal casing of the monitor. She then activated her wrist-phone.

"Jim?"

"Come in, Sophie. How did it go? Did he suspect you? Did you plant the device?" he asked.

"I did, it went okay. I don't think he suspected me. I put it where you told me to," answered Sophie.

"Get out of there now!"

"I will!"

Jim moved over to his computer, which he was not supposed to have or use, and checked to see if there were any readings. "Come on, Sophie, get out of there as quickly as you can!"

As Sophie was about to leave she heard Crawford calling her, "Sophie, come back to bed."

"I'll be there shortly."

Jim watched Sophie's biosignature on his computer monitor. He couldn't believe what he had just heard. Was Sophie going to sleep with Crawford and how could she have been even be thinking such a thing? He felt betrayed. He looked at the monitor once more to distract this kind of thinking that was slowly beginning to drive him crazy. "Come on, Sophie! Will you get out of there now!"

She went over to the main door to open it and found it was locked. Shock and fear were all over her face.

Jim watched with horror at the clock counting down from five to four seconds and knowing she was still at Crawford's apartment.

The clock hit one second and BANG!!!

There were an explosion and power throughout the biosphere was cut.

Crawford was not injured badly but had minor burning over his face and the rest of his body. The mainframe's user terminal blew up and Crawford soon realized what had just happened when he saw Sophie's badly burnt body beside the door.

CHAPTER TEN

There was widespread pandemonium across Apollo City in the wake of the explosion. Sears summoned Crawford to his Governor's Palace right away, instructing him to bring all he had on the Underground to him.

"Where are those damned files? I am going to wipe this revolutionary threat from this inept Underground before the week's out!" he yelled, determinedly.

He tapped the keys on the keyboard impatiently. Crawford was physically gauche. When he was a boy, he had the habit of banging himself against chairs and the edges of tables when he would get up after finishing meals. Struggling to be physically fit, he demanded things be done one way – the correct way. He tolerated no half measures from his staff or himself. He had a strong motivation to prove himself to Sears even though Sears held him in high regard.

He respected Sears and didn't want to oust him because he believed there was much to be learned from him.

"That bitch!" he yelled. "She must've put this there last night when I was in the bathroom. She was part of that damned Underground. How could I have been so stupid? I knew there was something about her," he said angrily.

He felt like the wool had been pulled over his eyes. He went outside his apartment block where his chauffeur was waiting for him. The driver greeted him and he responded with a grunt. He began to mutter to himself on the journey to his office. "How did I let her slip by? When Sears finds out what happened, he'll have my head on a platter."

They arrived at the Governor's Palace. It was constructed of marble and had the air of a temple to it. He nearly slipped when he got out and hit the door of the tram out of anger and pure frustration. He began to walk steadily to his study.

"Good morning, sir," said one official.
Crawford ignored him and kept on moving.
Other officials saw how forthright he was and tried to avoid passing him. He arrived at his office and entered it, slamming the door shut behind him. He quickly moved over to his desk and pressed a button on a communications console.

"Mister Clayton! Come to my office at once," he said, speaking into a small microphone. Crawford had just ordered his colleague, Clayton, the head of intelligence for the administration, to meet him as soon as possible since the incident. He was a staunch supporter of the Sears administration and appointed by Crawford recently. Crawford's secretary notified him that Clayton had arrived. He asked her to let him in. Clayton was as forthright as Crawford and displayed the same kind of dedication that he had. "Dean, you're just the person I need. Please sit," said Clayton, who was sitting at his desk with his arms out. Crawford sat down.

"How can I be of assistance to you, sir?" asked Clayton.

"That woman, Dean. Her name was Sophie Ramirez. I have compelling reasons to suspect that she was an Underground operative," he said while handing Clayton a picture of Sophie.

"How may I ask did you come to know this, sir?" asked Clayton.

"You certainly may ask, Dean. A member of the public informed us she was a subversive. I ran her name through our records and discovered she had received neuro-resequencing treatments."

"So she had an ax to grind?"

"I want you to fabricate evidence linking her to the Underground to tarnish their reputation," Crawford ordered.

"But what if she was innocent, sir?" asked Clayton.

"She was NOT innocent!" Crawford answered furiously. "We'll never curb this Underground threat if we play by the rules," continued Crawford.

"I understand completely, sir. I'll get right on it," said Clayton.

"Good, very good," responded Crawford with an arrogant grin.

Clayton made his egress from Crawford's office while Crawford himself began his daily routine of tasks such as studying reports on whether it was viable to construct another smaller biosphere alongside Apollo City.

CHAPTER ELEVEN

"I don't believe this. This is incredible," said Jim, who was studying the information he had received from the link between the transceiver and the mainframe computer. "They have files on us all... every citizen of Apollo City. Little do they know... I'd better hook it up again. This is very interesting." Jim connected the link again. "What's wrong? The link's broken." He reviewed the settings to see if there was a problem. "No, everything's as it should be. I hope Crawford hasn't discovered the transceiver!"

Jim moved over to the table and picked up his wrist phone. "Sophie! Sophie!" he said to it, but there was no answer. He typed in another code. "Richard!"

"Yes, Jim," answered Richard Barker.

"The link's severed. Can you find out what happened?"

"I'll get right on it. See you in one hour."

Richard was going to stop by the official offices to find out if Crawford had discovered anything. An hour had passed. Jim was working on his quantum computing device. He might be able to connect it to the mainframe computer to gain control of it. He didn't have all the information he required since the link between the transceiver and the mainframe was broken. The doorbell chimed. Jim walked over to answer it. He opened it to find Richard Barker, who was wearing a distraught expression. "Richard, what is it?"

Richard came inside. "Jim, I don't know how to tell you this," he said.

"Tell me what?" asked Jim. Richard didn't answer. "Damn it, Richard!"

"It's Sophie, Jim. They've killed her. She's dead. She didn't get out of Crawford's apartment in time. He made sure that he had the door locked, my sources say."

"What? That malevolent bastard!" said Jim, who was nearly weak. He sat down while tears came from his eyes. There was a moment of silence.

Richard put his arm around him. "I was never a people person. I was always a little deep. She was deep also and a beautiful and very good person. I am going to get those scum! No more being a pacifist! They're dead."

Jim dried his eyes with his fingers and said, "It's now or never!"

"What do you mean?"

"I mean today is the day we take over Apollo City! We have to do it now. Kill them all!"

"I don't know where you get your information from, but we're not murdering savages, Jim. We must continue with taking down the mainframe."

"Take down the mainframe? We need to do more than that! Give me weapons. I can get to them. I'll start by killing Crawford!"

"Hold on here! Nobody's killing nobody!"

"Just how in the hell do you expect to win this war, Richard? You have to get your hands dirty. It doesn't stop them from killing us!"

"When all of this is over, I'd like to say that I kept to my morals."

"It's not about morals. The administration has no morals. They're just murdering scum that we need to eliminate!"

"What the hell is wrong with you?! Don't you get it?! You think that's the most effective way. The true way a resistance should operate is a systematic, insidious breakdown of the administration piece by piece by disabling them technologically, little annoyances where vital, anything that inhibits their internal structure. No one has to get killed! That's what you always preached."

"Deep down when it comes to the crunch, I always thought it's about sharing the same pain the administration inflicted on me and everybody else on this rock — making them feel as miserable as we do. I don't have time for your textbook definition of what I am, Richard. They killed your wife, don't you remember?"

"I don't need reminding of that. Say we do it your way or at least some of it by your new found philosophy, maybe an eye for an eye."

Jim was about to respond only Richard became distracted at what he saw on the monitor. He began to study further the information which he had obtained from the link. Richard began putting together Jim's quantum computing device.

"I don't believe this!" Jim said, experiencing a crippling realization. "It's my fault she's dead. I knew she had no experience. I shouldn't have ordered her to plant that bomb."

"Wait!"

"What is it?" asked Richard.

"This is as good a time as any to test your equipment, Richard."

"It's all ready to go."

"Great. Let's initiate. If I'm right then none of this has to happen," Jim said with minimal enthusiasm.

"What are you talking about?"

"Time travel. If my calculations are right and I will adjust them accordingly, we can go back to yesterday and prevent Sophie's death."

Richard thought Jim was losing his mind. "Do you realize how crazy that sounds? I know you're grieving for Sophie, but the biosphere is in lockdown. We need to hide, Jim."

"No, we don't! I can undo this and maybe use

time travel to our advantage. You see, I still have these occasional bursts of knowledge – it's like if it is coming from somewhere else, I think the future. This could be what I am supposed to do – a message from my future self or future you."

"Bursts of knowledge like before the revolt? You came out with some weird crap. I thought you were just delirious back then but just say you could be right, why not just go back and make sure Sears is never made governor of Apollo City in the first place? That makes more sense!"

"I haven't got time or enough backup power to extend the long portal range through space and time. All I can do is go back a day or two. I need your help with the calculations. Let me make this right. Will you help me, Richard?"

"Just listen to yourself. You sound like a man obsessed!"

Jim thought for a moment and tears came from his eyes. "I supposed I am obsessed. I was obsessed with her and the thought of not being with her just made me want to lash out. That's why I continued with the Underground. It was just another way of ensuring that I got what I wanted – her but I will never know what's that's going to be like now.."

"I suppose I can help you, Jim. I have nothing to lose either."

They both began the quantum computing calculations needed to activate a portal. Using subatomic particles in a link in the form of an energy beam, Jim could open a vortex big enough to fit both of them, one by one, to enter it safely and hopefully come out in the past by two days. Jim knew that his actions couldn't be detected by conventional means. "These readings are strange. I'm going to use beam emitter to concentrate the energy beam on it. That should do it."

"What?" exclaimed Richard. "The beam has produced some negative energy."

"What's negative energy?"

"It's a form of energy that has an energy value of zero. It's not antimatter, which contains positive energy. I've never encountered it before."

"What the hell's that?" Jim asked at seeing the azure-colored distortion whirling concentrically in the room they were both in.

"That, Richard, is the distortion," said Jim, filled with deep fascination. "I don't believe it! It works – that's the portal!" Jim said fascinated.
Jim moved over closer to the distortion to study it further with a scanner that could scan the subatomic spectrum. The center of the distortion changed to a fuchsia blend of color.

"A portal to where and when?" asked Richard.

"Two days ago, Richard." Jim tried to tune into the vortex with the beam emitter. He adjusted it and discovered he could collapse it and re-establish it at will.

"How does the thing achieve this?" asked

Richard.

"The QBE, or, Quantum Beam Emitter, emits the energy beam to call up the portal at will. I can make it appear and disappear when I reactivate and deactivate the QBE."

More than surprise took Richard aback. Jim was ecstatic, a bittersweet ecstasy combined with grief and anger for Sophie.

"Is it dangerous?" asked Richard.

"It's completely safe. There's no radiation."

He adjusted the scanner accordingly. "Well let's do this. Let's make this right."

Richard decided to enter the portal first. As he was doing so, Jim noticed something on the monitor's readings that he could see located on the opposite side of the room. "Damn it! That won't do! Richard?"

Determined not to lose his only two close friends in such a short space of time, he followed Richard through the portal.

CHAPTER TWELVE

A green leaf blew across a large public park. The same vortex that pulled Jim and Richard into it reappeared in the park, but where and when was this? Moments later Jim and Richard were expelled with the same force that first pulled them in and which now landed them on the grass. There was nobody else around. They stood up. Experiencing natural sunlight for the first time dazed them.

"Where in the name of all that's holy is this place?" asked Richard.

"It looks like Old Earth," answered Jim.

"Could we have traveled back in time too far back?"

"It's possible. Are you all right?"

"I didn't break anything important. I can't believe we're experiencing natural sunlight."

The portal collapsed.

"Now we're stuck here!" cried Richard.

"Wait. I'll see if I can reactivate the portal with the QBE. There should be a subatomic link connecting Apollo City and here."

Jim pressed the emitter's controls. Within seconds the portal had been re-established. "I'd better collapse it again," he said.

"Why do you want to do that?" Richard asked, thinking Jim had lost it.

"Aren't you the least bit curious as to where and when we are right now? Richard, don't you realize what this means?" asked Jim.

"Yes, I do. We could maybe obtain help in some way for our Underground."

"This opens up many possibilities and options to us. Let's stick around and explore! And let's do it for Sophie."

They began walking around the park. They noticed an elderly couple sitting on benches. One of them was reading a newspaper. Luckily for Jim and Richard's sake, neither they nor the portal was discovered. "Look at the way they're dressed," said Jim.

"I've seen Old Earth attire before on file, and it looked nothing like that," said Richard.

Jim and Richard were dressed in light green Apollo City civilian uniforms. The elderly couple decided to go home and left the newspaper behind them. It got Jim's attention. They walked over to the bench, and Jim picked up the newspaper. The paper was The San Francisco Daily Digest. "It's a San Franciscan newspaper. We must be in California in the United States. This is weird!" Jim said after he looked at the date.

"Jim, what is it?" asked Richard, a little worried.

"It's the date. It says here it's August 20, 2015!"

"How could that be? The same day on Apollo City but Old Earth is a barren wasteland."

Jim began to think about this. "Richard, I don't think we have traveled back in time at all. I believe we have entered a parallel dimension or a different quantum universe."

"What do you mean?"

"I'll explain. The universe is part of a bigger multi-universe. Let's say that each universe is like a bubble in a boiling pot of water, and there's an infinite number of bubbles with each bubble representing a distinct quantum universe. The multi-universe can be described as the pot. We must've crossed the barrier between universes when we entered the portal and came out in a different distinct universe, where Earth and humanity have experienced a different path in history to ours."

"I wonder if there's an artificial biosphere on the moon here?"

"I guess we'll have to wait for nightfall to see if there is. I think we should find out as much as possible about this Earth as we can. Obviously, there was no asteroid attack like ours."

"What else does the information say on that paper?" Richard asked.

"From what I can make of it, the same as ours. The President of the United States is someone called Barack Obama and something about ISIS attacks in North Africa. This Earth is nothing like Old Earth," replied Jim.

"Jim, I don't think we should stay here for long in case we're discovered, and it seems this world is more chaotic than our own," said Richard with strong caution.

"This earth appears to be similar to ours over one hundred and fifty years ago, but ours was more advanced." Richard and Jim began to leave the park. As they were both walking off they saw a group of homeless people lying near bushes. "You would think a society this advanced wouldn't have people suffering like those," said Richard.

"It's the responsibility of every society to take care of everybody, especially the vulnerable. Otherwise there has to be organizations like my Underground to push for justice and equality like on Apollo City. I guess human beings here are just as obsessed with and out for themselves as the ones we're fighting against back home."

They were now wondering how they were going to blend in.

"We're going to have to dress like them. We can't go around here dressed in Apollo City uniforms," said Jim.

"What are we going to use for currency? How will we purchase food?"

"I'm not sure. I guess we'll have to improvise a lot."

They left the park and entered a busy downtown street, and as they expected, they received strange looks from people. Some were looks of bewilderment while others were humorous and derisive.

"Great! This is all I need. They think we're crackpots," said Richard, who was feeling obvious discomfort. Jim found it refreshing. "Wow! Look at those buildings," he said, referring to San Francisco's skyscrapers.

"Jim, this building is the San Francisco Public Library. This is the place where we can learn as much as possible about this Earth."

"Good thinking," said Jim. Jim's emotions were in turmoil. He was consumed with ever-deepening grief and anger at the loss of Sophie, a woman who meant the world to him, but at the same time, he had just made a groundbreaking discovery. The only thing that was keeping him together was his goal – overthrow Sears and to kill Crawford, thus in some way obtaining justice for her death. When they entered the library, they experienced obvious reactions to their incongruent attire.

"Jim, what are we going to do about our clothing? These uniforms are attracting too much attention." Jim looked at Richard, a look that was intended to instill reassurance.

"We'll stick around until we find something useful which we can use with our struggle. Then we'll get out of here as fast as we came.

Remember, Richard, the QBE can be activated at the touch of a button." Richard was not feeling more at ease.

"I sure hope the portal doesn't pull any of these natives back with us to Apollo City."

Jim and Richard walked over to the history section. This made the most sense to learn as much as possible about this Earth. Jim picked out a book entitled The Chronicles of the Twentieth Century while Richard picked out two smaller books on the nineteenth century.

"Let's get working. We've got a lot of research to do," said Jim. Nearly three hours passed by. They had finished perusing and flicking through their respective books and encyclopedias.

"The reason why this Earth is similar to ours over a century ago is that the industrial revolution and the pace and technological age began over a century later than on ours," said Richard with strong fascination.

"Different Earths follow different paths. The reason there's no biosphere on the moon is that Thomas Jenkins probably never existed here, and even if he did, his theories on supporting a biosphere on the moon wouldn't be realized with the limited technology available here right now," said Jim.

He was feeling an emotion that began with hopelessness and reached despair. "What can we really get from this world to help our cause?"

Richard was aware of what Jim was referring

to. "If you mean weapons that they have here."

"They murdered Sophie and your wife Abigail. They deserve to die!"

"If we go around planting bombs and killing everyone, we will end up opening up a Pandora's box that will ultimately destroy Apollo City."

"We could evacuate the citizens who want to come with us to some remote island on this Earth."

"Jim, that's a thought, especially if all else fails. Now I am going to read some books they may have on quantum physics. I might learn something new."

Jim walked over to the sciences section when an elderly man tut-tutted at him. Jim ignored him and smiled. He began to browse through the titles and noticed books by Einstein and Stephen Hawking. One book, in particular, took the ground from underneath him – his book entitled Fundamentals of Quantum Physics by James Callaghan. The book had a picture of the author who bore an exact likeness of him. He took it from the shelf. "Richard, come here... look at this."

Richard looked at Jim's picture and was in shock. "It's you, Jim," he said.

"Not quite. It's a picture of a parallel Jim Callaghan from this Earth. We must contact him. He can get us out of these clothes if nothing else."

"That would be great."

Jim's thinking began to charge like electrons in the atoms he once studied. He began to read his parallel self's biography note. "It might not be coincidence we ended up in San Francisco. Something my parallel self may be working on may have attracted the portal to this location. Going by the strict laws of quantum physics, we should have exited the portal at the exact same point as we entered it."

Richard nearly fainted when he heard this, and then he realized they could have ended up on the barren moon.

"We need to get in contact with him right away," said Jim.

"We can't just tell him, 'Hey, we're from another dimension,'" said Richard.

Jim looked at him and responded, "I know he'll understand."

Richard began to pace up and down, much to the discomfort of Jim. He noticed a group of people using computers a few rows away from them. He walked over to see what they were doing. He became amazed at the clicking and typing they were doing and even more perplexed at how consumed they were in their work. He picked out an elderly lady because she appeared less threatening for him to approach. "Excuse me, madam. Are these some kind of computing devices?"

The elderly lady didn't know whether to be amused or to be insulted at Richard's question.

"Where have you been for the last few decades? I'm logged on to the World Wide Web," she answered.

"My deepest apologies. You see, I am a foreigner to these lands. Can a person find out information on famous or renowned people using that interface?" he asked.

"You certainly can. I can find websites on everything and anything on this wonderful planet of ours."

"I see there is one free over there," said Richard.

"Is that how you dress in your country?" she asked.

"Oh, I work in the theater. I'm on my lunch break," answered Richard.

Jim read his parallel self's book closely. He thought if only he could meet with him. It would open up a whole load of possibilities. Some he could think of; others he couldn't begin to imagine.

"Jim!" Richard said softly. "There are computer interfaces where you can access what is called "websites" on anybody famous. We may be able to contact your parallel self."

Jim welcomed Richard's discovery. "Great work, Richard! Let's get right on it."

They moved over quietly trying not to draw any more attention to themselves than necessary. Jim sat down and carefully studied the keyboard layout and the Internet browser displaying on the monitor. The computers from this world were alien to him. He looked over at an attractive looking girl and watched how she was accessing information on the web. She was working much too fast for him to pick up anything. Richard noticed Jim was in difficulty. "I know someone who can help us with these computers," Richard told him.

He walked over to the elderly lady and asked her if she would mind coming over to show them how to log on. She was only too delighted to assist them. The elderly lady instructed Jim on how to call up a website. He took out the book written by his parallel self from his pocket and carefully covered the picture with his fingers and asked her, "I wonder how I could access a website on the author of this book? His name is James Callaghan. "

She showed Jim where to type that name into a search engine. Within seconds there appeared a hyperlink to James Callaghan's website. Jim clicked onto it and studied it carefully. The old lady returned to the workstation that she was using.

"This is just amazing. We know the same kind of knowledge. The same scientists on our Earth and this Earth must have made the same discoveries." He read the website further and discovered a bulletin board. He began to write up some threads which conflicted with the scientific reasoning underpinning the theories his other self had published. "My other self's mind alarmed when he saw what I have just written."

Richard didn't want to ask him what he meant because he knew he wouldn't be able to understand one word of it. A half hour passed by, and a response to Jim's thread was posted. He read it and was astonished. "It's from my parallel self, James Callaghan!" he said.

"What does it say?" asked Richard.

Jim turned to him and whispered, "It says my other self wants to meet the person who posted the threads which I posted - that he never heard of such theories before."

"This could be our chance, Jim. Tell him where we are." Jim couldn't type fast enough. "Don't worry. I intend to."

CHAPTER THIRTEEN

James Callaghan was at home in his apartment monitoring posts to his blog. He believed in making quantum physics easy to understand by all, so he could easily identify with the common man, which like Jim, had great difficulty. His website had a feature that explained scientific terms in plain English, and he used analogies to explain his theories. He was baffled at one particular thread. It had just been posted. This was the second out-of-the-ordinary occurrence he had experienced today. The other was a distortion he detected in the quantum spectrum. For the last two years, he had been trying to create a vortex with an Einstein-Rosen Bridge, which would be in essence a wormhole that would act as a means of transportation from one point of the Earth to another.

The only reason he wanted to achieve this was strictly in the interests of science. James was reluctant to share his discoveries with the military. He didn't want anything like that on his conscience. He read the latest thread and said to himself, "Who could have written this? It makes sense that quantum wormholes exist naturally, and we have to only attract them and amplify them to rupture out into our space and time continuum. I want to meet this person. If we could only achieve this together, it would bring my work closer by years."

He typed up another thread asking the person who wrote those theories if they could meet as soon as possible at his own expense. Within seconds he received a reply. "Great! They're still online, and they're in the San Francisco Public Library. I've got to get down there. Wait! Who wants to see me in the library of all places? This is some kind of trick, probably by someone in that inept science academy. They'll never allow me the opportunity to forget that I alone came up with those award-winning theories on quantum physics before they did. I will go to the library and find out what they're up to. They are not going to pull a fast one on me!" He locked up his apartment and headed for the elevator and said to himself, "Damn! I hate when I get this elated."

He entered the elevator and chose the ground floor. James Callaghan was as much of an erudite person as Jim Callaghan. He became impatient at little things like waiting in the elevator or being stuck in downtown traffic. He couldn't be bothered by ordinary everyday happenings. His mind played host to more exotic matters such as quantum physics and even his own theoretical temporal mechanics. He left his affluent apartment block and drove his car to meet the person who posted the theories on his website, which had taken him completely by surprise. He arrived at the library after avoiding traffic congestion. He thanked his lucky stars for that one. He hated being watched by other drivers or getting into possible road rage situations. "Now where and how to find this amateur! All I see is some man dressed in a jumpsuit. This better be a joke!" he said seeing Richard Barker dressed in his Apollo City uniform. Richard recognized him instantly as he was the same image and age as Jim. "Mister Callaghan," said Richard nervously. He was not used to seeing two of the same person.

"Are you him?" asked James, Jim's parallel self.

"Before you go in there, I need to explain something," Richard said, preparing James to meet himself in a few moments.

"My friend and I are not from this Earth."

"What?" James Callaghan asked.

"It's true," interjected Jim, who had just come out of the library.

"My God, you're some impostor," said James.

"No, I am you. I am as much you as you are me," said Jim.

"How?" asked James.

"We are from another dimension, a parallel quantum universe," Jim continued.

"Of course. But how did you end up here?" asked James.

Jim showed him the QBE. "I was conducting an experiment intending to time travel when I inadvertently ended up creating a portal between the boundaries of quantum universes, parallel realities of the universe."

"And then you ended up here?"

Jim nodded his head.

"Okay, but can you prove this?"

Jim reactivated the portal and as it appeared out of nowhere, James was mesmerized by its existence and efference.

"Wow!" James said as he moved closer to it.

"You shouldn't get too near the event horizon or it will pull you in!"

Jim collapsed the portal using the QBE and turned to his other self. "I need to know if you're conducting any kind of similar experiments like this, James?"

"I might be, why?"

"Just be straight with us."

"Don't you see – this is incredible! I've been trying to create a portal like this for the last two years. This could change the world!"

Richard looked at Jim. They both became dismayed.

James noticed how serious they were. "Why are you two so uptight? Yes, I have in operation a continuous scan of the subatomic spectrum... wait! That's why your portal was attracted to San Francisco and to this universe."

"This is all good and well. Could you get us out

of these clothes? We feel ridiculous. And could you give us something to eat?" asked Richard, who didn't want to hear any more technobabble.

"Of course. I wouldn't let myself or my friends starve. Come to my home."

They all got into James's car and made the journey home to his apartment.

"This is quite something. We've never experienced anything like this before – fresh air, motorcars or sprawling metropolises," Jim said.

"What kind of place is your Earth?" asked James.

"Our Earth is dead. We live on an artificial biosphere on the moon," answered Richard.

"Wow! What happened?" asked James with a curious fascination.

"An asteroid bombardment over fifty years ago," answered Jim.

"Our worlds are different. What are the chances of two James Callaghans existing in both universes when there are so many varied factors and circumstances?"

"It's astronomical," answered Richard.

"Or maybe it's divine intervention," answered Jim.

James began to prepare some food for Jim and Richard while they were changing into more appropriate clothing. James's apartment appeared to be something out of the 1950s. Jim and Richard didn't really notice any difference as everywhere on this Earth seemed alien to them.

James had an old style gramophone player with old 45s of Dean Martin and Frank Sinatra. James decided to cook some steak chops and put some music on. He took out one of Dean Martin's records and played "Amore." Jim and Richard were not sure whether to be captivated by the music or repelled by it. "What do you think, guys? Great music or what?" he asked.

"We've never heard anything like it before," answered Richard.

"Richard, it's similar to the controlled music Sears allows on Apollo City," Jim said.

"Apollo City. Why, the name itself evokes a fantastic space-age city on the frontier of the unknown. Do you go for a ride around the solar system in space ships?" asked James.

"We have limited fusion-powered ships that obtain ice from the Earth which we use as a source of water. As for traveling in outer space, it's just not viable," answered Jim.

"Living on the moon to us is just like living here for you – it's all we know, and we find it pretty ordinary," said Richard.

James walked into the kitchen to check on the steaks and vegetables. "They need a bit more time," he said.

He then went back out to join Richard and Jim. "I wonder how much we are alike," James said.

"You appear to me as a version of myself who is fulfilling his dreams and living your life freely. I, on the other hand, am struggling to find that place you're in right now," said Jim.

"What?" muttered James.

"Are you married, or do you have someone special?" he continued. "I've just lost someone who meant everything to me," answered Jim, who was feeling very lonely for Sophie. He was desperately trying to maintain his composure. He felt he must sort out Apollo City first and then grieve for her.

James couldn't wait any longer. "So let's see it!" he said.

"What? The portal?" asked Jim.

"Of course the portal. This could be the greatest discovery ever made. Do you know how long I dreamed of discovering something like this? I can't believe you discovered it by accident."

Jim took the QBE from his pocket and pointed it at an empty corner of the room. "Here it goes," he said. He activated it, and like before, the portal reappeared within seconds.

James moved closer to it and experienced the same kind of awe that Richard and Jim had experienced.

"Wow! What's it like going inside it?" asked James.

"It's like diving into a solarium," answered Jim.

"And we could go to your Apollo City right now?"

"Yes."

"How are you sure you will come out at the same point when you first entered it?" asked James.

"My quantum computing equipment first attracted the portal, so there's no reason why it shouldn't attract it again," answered Jim.

James turned to Jim with sincere appreciation and said, "If I can help you in any way, tell me. What do you need from me?"

"We may have to transport a lot of people through the portal. Let's just say Apollo City is less than hospitable right now," answered Jim.

"How many?" asked James.

"Thousands," answered Richard.

"Why here?"

"This planet is a paradise compared to Apollo City," answered Jim.

"You obviously don't know this world very well. It's far from a paradise," said James.

"If we fail, it might be our only option," said Jim.

"I'll do my best for you," James said sincerely.

Jim shut down the portal.

"So what's life like on Apollo City?" asked James.

"We will tell you more about Apollo City when the time's right," answered Jim.

"Perhaps I could go with you to see it first hand," said James.

"We'll let you know," said Richard.

Jim and Richard and the rest of the

Underground were involved in a struggle, and they did not want to complicate matters by bringing James back with them.

The Dean Martin record stopped playing.

"Thank you, Mister Martin, who always manages to entertain as wonderfully as ever. The reason why I'm so nostalgic for the 1950s is that it was a virgin time. Physics began to take off. The space age wasn't too far away. I sometimes wish I were around back then," said James with a deep sense of longing.

"On our Earth, these discoveries were realized over a century earlier by completely different scientists. Maybe they were meant to be discovered," said Jim.

"Wow! When it was the Wild West here, they were sending people to the moon on your Earth," said James, who was deeply intrigued.

"I wonder if I could take a look at your music collection," said Richard, who was feeling somewhat out of place by the two versions of the one person who were conversing about things he couldn't relate to. Richard flicked through James's record collection. He found it comforting to listening to the two dreamers who thought space and science were fantastic. He saw space as just another place to live. He began to flick over an album by Sinatra and discovered the picture on the sleeve of the next record was someone he knew very well. "What!" he said aloud.

Jim turned to him and said, "What's the

matter, Richard?"

Richard took out the album from the record rack and showed it to them.

"Where did you get this?" he asked James.

"That album is by Abigail Sumner. She's one of the few contemporary artists I listen to. I'm actually acquainted with her," answered James.

"You know her? Where is she now?" asked Richard.

"Wait, how do you know her?" asked James.

"She was my wife on Apollo City," answered Richard.

"Your wife?"

"I need to see her," demanded Richard. "I've been having dreams about her. This is some kind of destiny."

"Richard, we cannot afford to get into trouble on this world. It could be too risky," Jim said to Richard with the necessary authority.

"I really need to see her. Someone up there has set this up," said Richard.

Jim didn't want to force the issue. He knew if he had a chance to see Sophie again, he'd jump on it. James took the record from Richard, placed it on the gramophone and allowed it to play.

"I don't believe it. It's really her," said Richard.

"You must remember, Richard, she's not the same Abigail. She is what James is to me," said Jim.

"If I could just see her for one day at least. It would mean a lot to me, especially since it's our anniversary."

"Okay, Richard. I'll set up something," said James.

"Thank you," responded Richard.

"Now it's time for me to check the scans I've been doing." James went to his computer, which was interlinked with a device that scanned the quantum field in the local area. He was reading the latest data. "This is odd," he said.

"What is it?" asked Jim.

"There is some kind of aberration in the quantum field. I've never seen anything like it before. It's probably aftershocks caused by activating the portal. I'll look at it later," said James.

"How does it feel to be a respected scientist?" asked Jim.

"I can show people who are mostly idiots what I can do," answered James.

Jim became furious at his mirror self's remark and yelled, "How can you think like this?"

"Like what?" asked a baffled James.

"You know damn well what I'm talking about. You are like me a few years ago, except I had nothing. I had some entitling license to be a misanthrope. You, on the other hand, have everything that I aspire to have, and you're still miserable," answered an angered Jim.

"What can I do?"

"Do you not realize you are in a unique position to make a strong impact on your world and the people around you who think highly of you?"

"Yes, I suppose you are right." James began to think about what Jim had said and found himself agreeing with it.

CHAPTER FOURTEEN

James Callaghan, Jim's parallel self, was looking through the electronic phonebook on his PDA. He came across the number he was searching for. To his surprise he found it. "I've got it. It's right here," he told Richard.

"What exactly does that sequence of digits mean?" asked Richard, who had never seen or known anything about phone numbers.

James looked at Richard as if he were a man from another planet, and then he realized he was. "The digits represent a unique personal code. Each code or sequence of numbers identifies a person or business, etc," answered James.

Richard was now understanding this. He showed James his wrist phone and told him, "What I have wrapped around my wrist is also a communications device which transmits voice calls between people. It's similar to your 'telephone,' but uses our DNA to represent the calling parties." James began to have a closer look at Richard's wrist phone.

"Wow! I can't believe this kind of technology exists!"

"Oh, it's just one of the many idiosyncrasies of

Apollo City," Richard said, "Governor Sears being the weirdest of all. We'll contact Abigail now?"

James was beginning to feel somewhat uncomfortable, "We can't just call her up and say, 'Hey, I've got your husband from a parallel universe here with me, and he wants to meet you.' She'll think I am a right fruit cake," said James.

"I don't expect you to tell her that. I was going to a little later on," replied Richard.

"No way!" yelled James in a state of panic.

"Relax, Jim. I'm sorry, James. I was only joking."

"That's comforting," said a relieved James. Richard was wondering what Jim was doing.

"Where's Jim?"

"That's right. I'd better check on him," muttered James.

"What's Jim doing in that room anyway?" asked Richard.

"He's studying the aberration in the quantum field. It's probably nothing," answered James. He went into the room where Jim was and asked him what the current status was. Jim just shook his head with confusion.

James returned to join Richard, who was more than eager to make contact with Abigail. "So what's up?" asked Richard.

"It's tech talk; I don't recommend you listening to it if you don't understand it."

Richard didn't want to know after all. James took

his cellular phone out of his jacket and dialed Abigail's number. Richard now appeared like a man who was entering a state of manic stupor. He never thought he'd be going to see his beloved Abigail in the flesh ever again. James activated the speakerphone on his cellular and said, "Hi, Abigail. This is James Callaghan, the 'trippy scientist.' I have a DJ called Richard Barker who would very much like to interview with you for an up and coming radio station. Would you be interested? It would be great promotional stuff," said James.

"Sounds good. I would love to meet this Richard Barker. His name I don't know, but I think it means something," replied Abigail.

"Great, Abi. When can I set this up?"

"How about tomorrow afternoon?"

"Tomorrow afternoon sounds great. Thanks, Abigail," responded James, who pressed end call on his phone. He then looked at Richard, who had nearly turned white after hearing Abigail's voice again. She sounded as she always did to him. "I don't believe we're meeting her," Richard said with minimal lucidity.

"Guess it's all our lucky day."

"One thing though, what's a DJ?"

"That's something we have to work on."

When James was a teenager, he had aspired to be a disc jockey before he became fascinated with the sciences. He now had to prepare to give Richard a crash course in popular culture and his world's major communications medium – radio broadcasting. Two hours passed. Richard had almost been converted from an Apollo City freedom fighter to a twenty-first-century disc jockey. The two hours flew fast, and Richard was more than adept at his new subject and became a full-fledged disc jockey.

James had given Richard over a hundred dollars to pay for the meal and to tip the waiter. They arrived outside a country restaurant called The Bakers' Rest. Richard looked at James, "It's quite quaint, isn't it?"

"Quaint, it ain't. This is where all the big names in San Francisco showbiz hang out," said James.

"I don't know if I can see Abigail again," said Richard with growing uneasiness.

James tried to assuage his angst by buying him a malted scotch whiskey. "Here, this should help to pluck up your courage," he said.

Richard gave one look at the beverage and became even more anxious.

"Drink it down! It'll do you a world of good!" said James, whom himself was now also feeling a little of Richard's uneasiness.

Richard drank it down, coughed and nearly turned purple in the face. "What the hell was that?" he asked.

"It's old-fashioned Californian courage," answered James.

"I have to say I've never shared an alcoholic

beverage with Jim in all the days I've known him."

Richard took an observing view of the other people who were dining in the restaurant. To his shock and amazement, he saw the woman who was his wife on Apollo City. When Abigail walked in, she noticed James at his table and joined them.

"Abigail, it's an exhilarating pleasure as always," said James.

"The pleasure, as always, is mine. How are you, James?" she asked.

"I'm very well. This good man here is a very talented presenter of a new radio station which, as you people in showbiz say, is going to be very hot!"

"How do you do?" asked Abigail.

"Very good," answered Richard. He was not used to seeing his wife alive for one thing, but he was also not used to seeing her dressed in a lavish red dress.

Abigail sat down between them. She always required a person's undivided attention. "So how often will your radio station play my new single?" she asked Richard.

Richard gave a quick glance at James and said, "Standard playing time at first. Then as your song becomes more popular, which I'm sure it will, we'll be playing it as often as possible."

"That's great!" she said. James checked his watch and decided to leave Abigail and Richard alone, so he left the restaurant.

"It's just the two of us now," Abigail said with a smile that indicated she was enjoying being in Richard's company. The waiter took their order for venison.

"I've never tried venison before. I've heard lots about it," said Richard.

"I can assure you that you will be more than pleasantly surprised."

"So how long have you been a singer?"

"Since I was a very little girl. I was somewhat precocious. My brothers and sisters would turn the radio up to filter me out at times."

"I can't imagine they would do that. I must say you have the sweetest sounding voice I've ever heard... like a bird singing on a spring morning," said Richard as he remembered his Abigail and how he never really experienced a spring morning.

Abigail smiled and nearly blushed. "That's very kind and sweet, Richard. Thank you." They smiled and began to gaze at each other's eyes and laughed in unison.

"So how long have you known James?"

"I've known Jim for nearly ten years. He's a great leader," he answered.

"A leader?"

"I mean, as a friend. He leads me out of trouble."

Abigail laughed. "I don't think I want to know what kind of trouble you two get up to," she said jokingly.

"   It's all legal!" said Richard. For a second he thought he could have been explaining himself to an Apollo City official. He wasn't used to speaking to Abigail, and he still found it incredulous that different versions of her could exist in many parallel universes.

"So are you married, Richard?"

Richard always loved the direct approach Abigail had; however, he found himself put on the spot. "Ah, I used to be married," he mused.

"Sorry. I shouldn't have gone there."

"It's okay. It was some time ago. How about you?"

"No, I'm young, free and single."

The waiter served them their venison and they dined, mutually enjoying their choices.

"I think we should get down to the nitty-gritty on the launch of my single. Could your station do some kind of promo plug?" she asked as she became more serious.

Richard swallowed his portion. He did not know how to answer. "Sure. That shouldn't be a problem," he said.

They finished their meal and wrapped up their many topics of conversation, which they both enjoyed. Richard paid the bill and left a sizable tip for the waiter. They made a date to see each other the next day.

CHAPTER FIFTEEN

J ames returned from The Baker's Rest to his house to check with Jim on the status of the aberration they had discovered. He wondered to himself how Richard and Abigail would get on and if it would be everything Richard wanted in a surprise reunion. He joined Jim, who was glad to see his more successful self. To Jim, it was like having an extra self to delve into for answers and expertise he could not come up with. The readings from James's PC had perplexed him, and James could not have come home at a better time. Jim needed to ask him to look at the latest readings.

"I don't know how those two will hit it off, but I'm sure they will," said James, still thinking about Richard and Abigail.

"We can talk about that later. Right now we've got a problem on our hands," responded Jim.

"What kind of problem?"

"I'm not quite sure. It's like the subatomic particles and the entire quantum field are going through a state of flux."

James looked at the readings more closely.

"   If this continues, the effects will emerge out into the living and breathing world. We've got a major problem on our hands," said James, alarmed and worried.

Jim looked at the data again. "It's like a quantum virus. I think Richard and I have caused this."

"How so?" asked James.

"Richard and I are from a completely different universe to this. Not just different historically or socially but also unique in the makeup of its quantum field. Each universe has its own unique quantum field. When we entered your universe, we interfered with that unique makeup and caused subatomic chaos."

James took a deep breath, "You've inadvertently created a subatomic virus. God only knows what this will mean."

James began to pace up and down and asked, "How far is this virus progressing?"

"It's incipient, but it will accelerate."

"By these readings, the entire San Francisco metropolitan area has been infected. We have to find a way to counteract it fast."

"Richard and I must return to Apollo City and bring back some of my equipment. With luck, I should be able to eradicate the virus."

"And if you're not successful?"

"I don't think there should be a problem."

"Just how do you know all this stuff. It would take me years."

"I'm not sure you will believe me?"

"Trust me. Talking to my real life reflection like now – I'll accept anything."

"One day I was leader of the Underground trying to topple the regime when I remembered the future. So I got Richard to realize my theories – he's very good at creating things – and I try to attempt going back in time only to arrive here instead."

"I only remember the past."

James finished the conversation while a quantum physics book caught his eye. He nudged Jim on his right shoulder. "You know, Jim. I think the knowledge you got from the future came from that book. I think you should read it before we go home to keep the causality cycle running in the right direction otherwise the causality cycle will break apart thus destroying the universe."

Jim picked up the book and opened it and began perusing it. To his astonishment his counterpart was correct. "It's like I read this book before. How is this even possible?"

"Not sure but read as much of it as possible."

Eight hours passed and he consumed the book with his best effort. He was about to yawn when James shoved a mug of coffee in front of him. "This should keep your eyes open, Jim."

Jim thanked him and drank it down almost in one good gulp.

James's doorbell chimed. He answered it to

find a lovesick Richard Barker.

"Richard, we've got to get out of here as soon as possible. We're going home," said Jim.

"What... today?"

"As soon as we can."

"But I have to see Abigail tomorrow. If I don't, it could ruin everything."

"I'm afraid, Richard, we don't have a choice."

Jim explained the discovery of the quantum virus to him. Richard had never cared for quantum physics. He placed his complete trust in the two selves of the soon to be eminent scientist called Jim Callaghan.

"Can I just have one day? It's imperative that I see Abigail again. For the first time since her death, I feel alive," implored Richard.

James looked at his mirror self and said, "We all need more time to learn more about this virus. It's in its early stages. Another day won't hurt."

Jim agreed and took pity on his valued friend.

CHAPTER SIXTEEN

Richard went to the park where he and Jim had first entered this universe. He had arranged to meet Abigail there. He looked around and found himself enjoying the fresh air once again. He particularly watched young couples in love walking by. All he ever wanted was to find the right woman and raise a family that would one day live on Earth, or at least their descendants would, with a woman like Abigail. But just like Jim's Sophie, she was so brutally taken from him. Now that he'd found her again, he felt she wanted the same in due time. Abigail arrived dressed in a white t-shirt and blue jeans. They greeted each other with warm smiles.

"It's good to see you again, Abigail," he said.

"It's only been a day."

"You don't know how long a day can be when you're waiting to spend the next one with someone special."

Then he almost wished he hadn't said it, or at least said it like that. Abigail just brushed it off. They went for a walk around the park, not hand in hand, although Richard made that attempt only to find Abigail wouldn't entertain that. He thought she may have been embarrassed.

"What did your radio station think of my record?" she asked.

"They loved it and said you are a natural, which you are."

They kept walking and stopped by an ice cream stand. Richard, who had seen a picture of a large ice cream cone, ordered two with lots of strawberry sauce on each. He gave the kid at the stand ten dollars and told him to keep the change.

"You radio people like to splash out, don't you?" said Abigail.

"We like to spread happiness. It's good to spread happiness."

"You said you were married once. Was it a good marriage, if you don't mind me asking?" A bittersweet feeling of sadness combined with joy-filled Richard's heart.

"She was the most beautiful person I have ever known. She had the voice of an angel. She'd sing for hours on end. I was captivated by her when I first saw her. When I first heard her sing, I was under her spell."

"Wow! She was a singer like me. I wonder if I've heard of her?" she asked.

Richard answered her question with a smile. They left the park two hours later and went to the movies, where they watched a romantic picture. Richard didn't pay much attention to the movie, but Abigail was enthralled with it. It was night now, and Richard was nervous about the time factor regarding his re-acquaintance with Abigail and having to re-join Jim. He knew he and Jim had to return to Apollo City tomorrow, and he was feeling tired. He wanted to spend the night with the woman who was once his wife, but he constantly had to remind himself that she wasn't his wife.

"Let's go to the club where I perform," Abigail stated.

"I can't. It's very late."

"We'll just have a few drinks. We will only spend an hour at most there."

"Okay so."

They got into her car and headed for her club. It wasn't far from downtown San Francisco. When they arrived at the club called The Siren Room, Richard yawned and escorted Abigail inside. The man at the door instantly recognized Abigail and welcomed them both in. Richard was behind Abigail when he saw the interior of the club. He nearly fell dead! It was the exact same smoky club he had seen in his dream a few nights earlier on Apollo City. The shock hit him as if he were traveling through the portal that brought him to this world. He now knew there was something inexplicable behind all of this and that he and Abigail were destined to be together. Up until now, he didn't want to push it, but now he felt the time was right. He decided to be direct because she always preferred the direct approach. They ordered cocktails. Richard was becoming quite fond of alcoholic beverages. They watched Abigail's close friend, Caroline, perform. She spotted Abigail in the audience and asked her to do an impromptu duet with her. Abigail agreed. When Abigail was singing with Caroline, Richard felt as if his dream had come true in the literal sense. She sang the same song that was in his dream, or at least it sounded like it. He couldn't remember exactly. He felt the time was right for him to make his move; he'd do it when she returned to their table. A few minutes later Abigail finished her duet with Caroline and re-joined him.

"What did you think?" asked Abigail.

"You were great as always," answered Richard. "Have you seen me perform before tonight?"

"In a way I have."

"I think I'll leave it at that," she replied.

Richard felt this was the right moment to pursue his direct approach. "Abigail, how do you feel about us getting to know each other better? I think we would be great for each other. Do you agree?"

Abigail was taken aback. "I'm sorry, Richard. I'm afraid I can't get to know you better."

"Why? I don't understand."

"I got married last month to my lifelong partner. We decided to keep it secret for a while because our ceremony was in Bermuda. That's why I said I was single before. I'm really sorry, Richard," she answered.

"Oh! I'm the one that's sorry. If you will excuse me, I'd better be off."

He got up and took one last look at Abigail and went outside. He hired a cab for him to return to James's house. On his way back he thought the universe had played a big practical joke on him. He was angry and wanted to get off this world as soon as possible.

CHAPTER SEVENTEEN

J im and Richard said their goodbyes to James. They returned to the park where they first came to this universe. Some people passed them, and this prevented them from using the QBE. They decided to wait for nightfall to make their return back to Apollo City. Jim was feeling the loss of Sophie heavily. He knew when he arrived back on Apollo City she would not be there. He found meeting his alter ego a welcome distraction, and he looked forward to returning here to see if James would have changed in some way. This was also a time that would test Jim Callaghan as leader of his self-designed Underground. He knew he had to get justice for Sophie and intended to do so as soon as he found a way to curb the aberration in the quantum field. The loss of Sophie, who had instilled a new meaning into his outlook on life and gave him a surge of confidence, meant that he was in danger of reverting back to his old ways of thinking.

Seeing people of this world who generally seemed to be carefree and indifferent also made him resent them a little. He found it better to keep himself distracted. He was on a roll and enjoyed it perversely. "Richard, I'm trying desperately to like that version of me," he said.

"You mean James?"

"Yeah, James."

Richard looked at Jim and said, "Now it's my turn to display my frailties. When the hell will it be the right time to get out of this tantalizing, crazy, self-serving world?" he asked.

Jim saw the anguish in Richard's eyes and noticed only too well his discomfort of the entire evening.

"Easy, Richard. Another twenty minutes should do it," Jim replied.

"Twenty minutes too long! I hope you won't be surprised to know that I won't be returning to this damn planet again with you."

"Fine. None of us will be if I don't cure this virus."

"Why don't we just leave it? They're not us. They're just carbon copies of us, mere clones."

Jim nearly fell dead when he heard what Richard had just said.

"What do you mean? They're living, breathing sentient human beings like us, and I don't want the destruction of an entire universe on my head."

"Yeah. You're right, Jim."

Richard was still feeling cheated on the business with Abigail. He thought after she told him she was married that everyone on this Earth was a fraud. Twenty minutes passed by, and the park had become less populated. There was now a window of opportunity, and Jim decided to take advantage of it. He pressed the appropriate button on the QBE to reactivate the portal. It appeared as glorious as ever, and they allowed themselves to be drawn by its gravitational pull into it once more.

They arrived back in Jim's apartment at exactly the same spot where they had left Apollo City. Something was different though; all of his belongings and quantum computing equipment were gone. Had Crawford discovered that he was the leader of the Underground in their absence? Jim wanted to find out while Richard was just delighted to be home.

"We've got to find out what has happened here while we were gone. Without my equipment, the universe we just left will be destroyed," said Jim, with a strong sense of urgency.

"What can I do to help?" asked Richard.

"Contact our people. Find out what went on. Report back to me in an hour. I'll be in my usual hiding place."

Jim quickly hid the QBE and made his way to his hideaway. He avoided the guards that were outside his apartment block. They almost spotted him. Jim arrived at his secret hideaway, an unused warehouse with a basement. It was located at the north rim of Apollo City. There was no one else there. He found himself some food and a small pocket-sized computer that Richard Barker once made for him. He switched it on, but it didn't work right. He looked to his amazement at the readings. They were conveying something, but he could not figure them out because the computer wasn't working properly. He switched it off and began to prepare himself some food. The last time he had eaten was at James's house. He heated up a pasta-based meal and ate it.

He had to stop eating when he heard people coming. He hid behind a stack of old computer monitors. Three people came in. He could not make out who they were because it was dark. They came closer. He noticed their uniforms were a different color. Instead of being light blue, they were light green. He heard a woman speak. Her voice was a lot like Sophie's. She came closer. It was Sophie! Jim got out from hiding and rushed out to see if it was really her. "Sophie! Sophie!" he said.

Sophie took out a weapon that was strapped to her waist and pointed it at him. "It's another impostor," she said to a man.

The man came closer. It was Richard. Jim saw another man behind him who was pointing a weapon behind Richard. The man behind Richard was also Richard!

"Who are you?" asked Sophie.

"I am Jim Callaghan. I am the leader of the Underground."

"You can't be. Jim Callaghan was executed two days ago. I saw him die with my own two eyes," said Sophie.

"I'm telling you that I am as much Jim Callaghan as he was. Let me explain."

"Go on then. Humor us."

"You know the experiment that I, your Jim Callaghan, was working on?"

"Yes."

"I was working on it too. I discovered a means of traveling from one quantum universe to another, each slightly different from the other. Richard, who has a gun pointed at him, and I are from another quantum universe."

"We're supposed to buy that? You are impostors intent on infiltrating the Underground," said the alternative Richard Barker. Sophie looked at the alternative Richard and said to him, "What if they're telling the truth? It would explain that thing Jim created before Crawford and Clayton came to execute him."

"Was that a blue distortion... a vortex?" asked Jim.

"Yes," answered Sophie.

"That was the portal we used to come here. We thought this was our Apollo City. Let me show you."

Jim took out his QBE and activated the portal. It appeared. Sophie and the alternate Richard were almost speechless.

"That was it!" she said.

"Now would you kindly stop pointing that damn weapon at me? I've gone through enough today," said Jim's Richard to the alternative Richard, and he did.

Sophie and the alternate Richard began to believe them, and they all sat down and had drinks.

"I can't understand why you were carrying weapons. I would never sanction that unless we were in direct combat," said Jim, referring to Sophie and her Richard's weapons.

"We are in direct combat," yelled the alternative Richard.

"We declared direct combat when our Jim was killed. I'm the leader of the underground now," said Sophie.

"You're the leader of the Underground?" asked Richard.

Sophie didn't have time to answer because her attention, as well as the attention of the two Richards, was grabbed when they discovered distortion and melding of the stack of computers. Jim went to investigate it.

"What the hell's going on?" asked Sophie.

"It's all stuck together... the computer monitors and the thin air that surrounds them," said Jim's Richard.

"It's the quantum virus. Our presence here in this universe has caused this. The virus is moving at a more accelerated pace here than on the universe we just left," answered Jim.

"How can we stop it?" asked Sophie.

"We've got to get my equipment back," said Jim to Sophie.

"We can try. We'll need your help. Explain more about the virus," said Sophie.

"It is caused by subatomic particles reacting with the subatomic particles that are from outside your universe, which Richard and I brought here from our own universe and from the universe that we just left. This virus is causing all matter to meld together on a molecular level," Jim explained.

"Does this happen to each universe you enter? They each become infected?" asked Sophie.

"Yes, there is possibly an infinite number of parallel universes, an infinite number of infections."

They quickly devised a plan to get back some of Jim's equipment so he could study the virus further.

"Look!" said Sophie. She showed them the distortion, the virus. It had an effulgence about it. It was beautiful. Everything was melded together and radiating brightly.

"It's beautiful," remarked Jim.

"Beautiful? We could all be melded together like that," said Jim's Richard.

"He's right. We'd better get moving," ordered Sophie.

The two Richards went out first. Jim looked

into Sophie's eyes and had a good look. He thought he would never have that opportunity again. She was practically identical to his Sophie except for the variation in the color of the uniform.

"You make a good leader," he said.

"Wasn't I always your first woman and your second in command?" she asked.

Jim laughed sarcastically, "You were my only woman. The only one who ended up betraying me."

She didn't know how to respond to that remark and brushed it off. Jim and Richard changed their uniforms to that of the alternate Apollo City's. They walked to the government police barracks, where the parallel Sam Crawford had confiscated the parallel Jim's equipment. There were four guards patrolling the barracks. Jim knew they had to be taken down, and before he could have said that, Sophie had ordered it to be so. She aimed at the first guard and fired. Jim fired his weapon at the second guard. He hit his target. Sophie missed her target, and the guard fired back. She ran across and fired again and got him. The two Richards, who were hiding behind a wall at the back of the building, fired at the two remaining guards. They fired back and hit the alternative Richard. He was dead. Jim's Richard fired four shots and hit the two of them. He ran to the back entrance and went in and called Jim on his wrist phone. When the three of them met up inside, Richard told them that Sophie's Richard hadn't made it. They found Jim's equipment inside. Jim picked out his alternative self's scanner, which was another handheld device and a fully working pocket-sized computer.

"I've got everything. Let's go!" he said.

The alarm went off. They quickly left the building and headed for a public tram, which they entered quietly. Jim turned on his scanner and used the password. Luckily it was the same. He began a scan of the quantum field. Deep concern ran from his head to his heart. Sophie noticed Jim's unease.

"What is it, Jim?" she asked.

"The virus. In three hours your Apollo City will be totally melded. You've got to come with us back to the parallel Earth where we just came from. I've got to give this equipment to my alternative self."

"I can't. I'm needed here."

"We can't do much for here right now. We'll have to get back and sort this Apollo City out later," said Jim.

They got off the public tram and walked into a quiet corner. Jim took out his QBE and pointed it to an empty corner and pressed it on. The portal began to reappear, but it too was distorted. The virus had disrupted its cohesion.

"Damn! It won't work," cried Richard. "I can't get it to form properly. I'll have to amplify the quantum beam," said Jim.

"There's no way I'm going inside that. We'll all be spaghetti," said Sophie.

Jim pointed the QBE at the crumbling vortex, and it emitted an amplified quantum beam, which did stabilize it nicely. Moments later, after all three of them were instantly pulled into it, it collapsed. Where they were going to end up was anyone's guess.

CHAPTER EIGHTEEN

The portal reappeared against a scenic backdrop that could easily be used as a picture postcard. Everything appeared clean, opulent and pristine. No pollution, just fresh air. There was a cityscape visible in the background with trees and fresh green grass in the foreground. Jim, Sophie and Richard came out of the portal. They appeared disorientated due to the effects of the virus and increased amplification of the vortex. Sophie looked at Jim and Richard and asked, "Where are we?"

"I don't think we landed on our desired destination," answered Jim.

"Not another parallel universe! We've got to get out of here as fast as we came here and keep trying to get to James's Earth," said Richard.

"You're right, Richard. We'll go right now," said Jim.

"I can't believe it! The air here is even purer and cleaner than on James's Earth," said Richard.

"Wait! What is that?" interjected Sophie.

She was referring to a distant moon-like planet which she saw from Earth's sky. Jim and Richard looked to where she was pointing and shared her amazement and astonishment.

"It's another planet in this Earth's solar system," answered Jim.

"It's freaking me out. Let's get out of here right now," cried Richard.

"We will. We've got a lot of work to do. But first I must discover what trail we may have left behind us to find the same path back to James's Earth and home," Jim said as he took out his pocket-sized computer and interfaced it with the QBE.

"I might be able to tune the quantum beam to follow the unique structure in each universe's quantum field and use it as a path of breadcrumbs, so to speak," Jim continued. Just as he was about to carry this out, two people appeared out of thin air in front of them and were pointing weapons at them.

"You are all under arrest," said a female guard. She fired the gun at Jim, Sophie and Richard. It didn't kill them. Instead, an energy field surrounded them, and they all vanished.

"Where are we?" asked Sophie, who was referring to the cell where she, Jim and Richard were confined. The cell was triangular in shape and was completely made up of energy fields, which acted as force fields.

"I think we're in some kind of holding cell. They know we're not from their universe," answered Jim.

"Did you see that "thing" in the sky? What is it?" asked a perplexed Richard.

"It seems to be a small alien planet that's present in this Earth's solar system. I've always wondered if life existed elsewhere in the universe, and evidently it does in this universe, right on Earth's doorstep. I wonder if we will meet any of them," answered Jim.

"We've got to get out of here any way we can," said Sophie.

"They have the QBE. Let's just wait and see what they want from us," replied Jim.

They waited patiently for over three hours. Then a group of five guards came along the corridor escorting an African-American official. They arrived at the holding cell and switched off the force field. "I am Al Hudson. I am the First Prelate of the UWEN, The United Worlds of Earth and Nartania. We have identified you as alien intruders from another dimension or a completely different universe. In fact, two of you originate from the same universe while the woman comes from yet another distinct universe. Are you at all aware of the repercussions you have caused by coming to this world?"

"You mean the virus?" asked Jim.

"You know about it?" asked Hudson.

"We are trying to fix it," answered Jim.

Hudson laughed and said, "You fools, don't you realize what kind of fire you are playing with?"

"We have a good idea, and if you release us, we can get back working on it," said Sophie.

"How do we know that you did not come here deliberately to infect our two peaceful worlds? Perhaps it's a prelude for an invasion?" asked Hudson.

"Invasion! Do we look like marauders?" laughed Richard.

"We will formally interrogate you presently. In the meantime, we will reverse the damage you have caused to this universe's quantum field."

"No!" yelled Sophie as she became enveloped by and melded by the same effulgence that occurred on her world.

"What's happening to her? You've got to stop this," demanded Jim.

Hudson instructed his guards to take Sophie away, much to the dismay of Jim.

"Where are you taking her?" he asked.

"She will be placed in an isolation chamber where her complete subatomic structure will be reconfigured so as to adapt to this universe," answered Hudson.

"You can do that? You have a cure?" asked Jim.

"Not quite. However, it prevents the spread of the virus. You and your friend must also undergo this treatment."

"So you're beginning to believe us?" asked Jim.

Hudson didn't answer. He walked back out of the holding cell. Two aliens placed Sophie in stasis. She was floating in mid-air. They applied an energy field which surrounded her. On a monitor, her DNA could be seen. It appeared distorted. One of the aliens placed a device over her body. It emitted an energy pulse. On the monitor, the image displayed her DNA being reverted back to normal at the subatomic level. The shining melding began to dissipate, and within minutes she was a normal, sprightly and healthy young woman once more. Jim and Richard also underwent this process. They no longer were a threat to this universe. They were given food, a bath and a change of clothing. Jim, Sophie, and Richard were seated outside on a veranda, which was set against a vast garden containing Earth flowers as well as alien flowers from Nartania. Jim and Richard appeared serene. Sophie was somewhat unsettled.

"What's the matter?" Jim asked, turning to Sophie.

"When I was melded, all my thoughts were paused. All I could think of was the same thing over and over again. It was hell! There was something trying to speak to me, sending me horrible historical mental images of all the bad things human beings do."

"What kind of bad things?" asked Jim.

"Murder, rape, mutilation of people, pure evil."

"It's over now, at least for us. We've got to get their help in eradicating the virus on your Apollo City and on James's, my alternate self's, Earth.

Otherwise, it will be an infernal experience for all of them. I wish I knew how they achieved the cure."

"How can you be sure they will help us?" asked Richard.

"I think they believe us. Let's just give them some time."

They relaxed for a while and enjoyed graciously the refreshments they were given.

CHAPTER NINETEEN

Al Hudson had just joined Jim, Sophie and Richard. They were feeling rested but anxious about solving the virus.

"Jim, could I have a word with you? We need to talk," said Hudson.

Jim agreed and became very interested in what Hudson had to say. They entered some kind of transporting booth and were teleported. The destination transportation booth opened, and Jim and Hudson were now on the planet Nartania. The leader of the Nartanian greeted Jim.

"Where am I?" he asked.

"Look over there... that's Earth!" replied Hudson.

"Wow!" said Jim.

The planet Nartania was filled with unusually shaped cities like shining frosty diamonds scattered on clay that were raised miles upright from the ground, and the sky was light pink in color. Hudson and Jim walked to a room. Jim sat down while Hudson and the Nartanian alien stood.

"Allow me to tell you a story, Jim, if I may?" he asked.

"Certainly," replied Jim.

"This planet Nartania we are on right now did not always exist in this, my universe. About one hundred and sixty years ago it appeared in our universe through a natural cosmic disaster or event. No one knows how this occurred. Nartania appeared exactly at the same point in space that it had occupied in its own universe where life on the Earth indigenous to that universe never existed. At first, there was widespread panic on my Earth when an alien celestial moon-like object appeared in the sky. Peaceful contact was made, and our two races began to trust each other. About one hundred years later, both worlds formed The United Worlds of Earth and Nartania."

"If the planet Nartania came from another quantum universe, then the virus would be present. The Nartanian found a cure?"

"Right. Yes, they did. They discovered it, studied the virus and found a way of eradicating it by using a subatomic shockwave. The same shockwave was used on you and your two friends."

"Are there any Nartanian people left now?"

"No, Jim. They all were dying and became extinct eighty years ago."

"You must help us!"

"I am not sure it's our place to go interfering

with the laws of the universe. We are reluctant to share their technology with anyone," said Hudson.

"Just reconfigure my QBE to trace back our footsteps and to enable it to fire the subatomic shockwave. Otherwise millions will suffer horribly," pleaded Jim.

"I will do my best, my friend."

Jim paced up and down along a corridor. He rejoined Sophie and Richard back on Hudson's Earth. He was waiting for Hudson's decision.

"Do you think they will help us?" asked Richard.

"I hope so," answered Jim.

"I certainly don't want to stay here for the rest of my life," said Sophie.

They heard footsteps. It was from Hudson.

"Well, will you help us?" asked Jim.

"You are all in luck. It took three hours of debating, but we will help you. We have reconfigured your QBE as Jim asked. It will take you back to each of the quantum universes where you have already visited. When you are there, just press this button to activate the subatomic shockwave."

"Great! We're going home," yelled Sophie.

Hudson looked at Jim and Richard with sadness and then turned to Sophie. "I'm afraid the quantum universe where you originated from cannot be saved. The virus is far too complex even for our technology to solve," said

Hudson.

"What do you mean? I can't return home?" asked Sophie.

"No, I am afraid not. Some quantum fields in some universes become very infected by the virus. Your universe falls into that category," answered Hudson.

Tears came from Sophie's eyes. Jim placed his arms around her and said, "Come to my Apollo City. I need you there, and I need you in my life." She nodded and hugged him. Jim switched on the portal, and as before it pulled them into it.

CHAPTER TWENTY

Jim, Sophie and Richard arrived back on Jim's alternative self's Earth and were near James's home in San Francisco. Jim told Sophie not to be perplexed when she saw yet another version of himself – James. She told him that nothing surprised her anymore. "Okay. It's time to initiate the subatomic shockwave," said Jim. He pressed the switch that Hudson showed on the altered QBE, and a transparent energy pulse was fired from it.

"That's it? That's the cure?" asked Richard.

"That's the cure," answered Jim.

They walked for over forty-five minutes to James's home. Once again they received looks and laughter from people because of the attire they were wearing; however, this did not bother them in any way. They arrived at James's home, and Jim rang the doorbell. The door opened, and James greeted them exclaiming, "The virus, Jim ... it's gone!"

"I know. We found a cure. Let us in, and we'll tell you all about it," said Jim.

Jim told James all about Hudson and the

Nartanian. James was simply astounded.

"Who are you?" he asked referring to Sophie.

"I'm with your other self, Jim," she answered.

"I'm very happy for you both. Richard, would you like to meet up with Abigail again?" asked James.

"No, James. I think I'll leave her be. It's time that I put her to rest," answered Richard.

Richard did not feel like having the universe, or worse still, the multi-verse playing any more tricks on him. He also felt it was time for him to move on. James provided them with showers and prepared them with a hot meal and a change of clothing. Sophie and Richard went into another room where they discussed the differences in their respective Apollo cities as Jim instructed them to do.

Jim and James were in James's workroom studying this universe's healing quantum field. "You know, Jim, I don't think I can ever get used to looking at my reflection, which is you. What I am trying to say is I took you up on your words you had with me when you were last here, and I have begun to change my ways. Maybe there's a Sophie on my Earth that I could look up. You never know," said James.

"I'm glad to hear that. It's not easy looking at your negative points in a person that's a carbon copy of yourself," replied Jim.

"I know." They talked and laughed for a while. Richard and Sophie joined them. They had some drinks, and all fell asleep.

The next morning it was time to say the final goodbye to James. It was a deeply emotional moment for Jim and even Sophie. Richard felt uncomfortable on this Earth. Jim reactivated the QBE, and just like clockwork, they were gone. James smiled. He literally positively saw himself and now knew there was a different way of thinking.

CHAPTER TWENTY ONE

J im and Sophie were flung from the vortex. The unusually vehement pulsating light emanating from the vortex's event horizon almost blinded them. It was clear in Jim's mind that something went wrong during transit. They both opened up their eyes or at least tried to. Each of them could not see clearly at all.

"Sophie, are you all right?"

"Don't worry about me. I'm tougher than you. Is the trip to Hayes's reality always this bumpy?"

"No. Even though Richard and I landed here by accident, it was a much more pleasant ride. The vortex was warm. Funny, it's been always average temperature."

"It was very hot. There must be something wrong. I can barely see properly."

"Me too."

They began to hear footsteps from more than one person. These people sounded like they were walking steadily down a long corridor. A door opened with a piercing, strident noise.

"You two, stand up straight now!" a harsh, authoritarian male voice said.

Jim and Sophie, whose balance had been lost, were crouching. They became bewildered and carried out this man's orders.

"You don't understand, I personally know Hudson!" Jim implored.

"I know you do," a man attired in armor and a mask replied sarcastically.

"Guards, bring them to the cell. He'd be glad of the company after all of these years!"

Two human guards grabbed Jim and Sophie. Sophie resisted only to be zapped by an electroshock gun.

"Leave her alone!" Jim yelled.

The guard zapped him also.

Jim and Sophie were escorted to a cell. The other guard pulled a hatch open followed by the cell's door. The guard who was forceful with them shoved Jim and Sophie into the cell. Sophie landed on her hand. She yelled with pain. Her hand was braised and Jim extended out his to gently massage it. She pulled it away from him quickly.

They noticed an old man who had been sleeping on a rangy bed looking with wonder at them. He couldn't believe his eyes. He became fixated at the emblems of Apollo City on each of their jumpsuits that featured the biosphere.

"Are you really from there? Is this more

torture?" he asked them.

"Just where do you think we're from, sir?" Jim asked.

"The biosphere, of course."

"How do you know about where we came from?"

"I'll tell you because I'm from Apollo City too. My name is Thomas Jenkins."

"What?!" Sophie said. "Thomas Jenkins died a long time ago on my Apollo City. How about yours, Jim?"

"He reportedly died months after the asteroid bombardment."

"Don't tell me you are each from a different, distinct version of the same biosphere? This means you are capable of traversing the multiverse."

Jim moved over closer to Jenkins. "How'd you end up here? I take it Sophie and I are not in the world that was our intended destination? I'm Jim Callaghan, by the way."

Jenkins had a brief moment of confusion that was followed by a slight realization. "No. You're prisoners like me here, like all humans except for a chosen few who sell their souls. Prisoners of the Nartanian."

"You know, Mister Jenkins, I was recently on a world where humanity and the Nartanian coexisted peacefully and cooperated with each other. The opposite must be true here."

"That is the varying nature of the multiverse.

No two situations or people are that similar. You said your name is Callaghan?"

"Yeah, that's right."

"Is your mother called Sandra?"

Jim was surprised that he knew his mother. "Yeah, that was her name but both of my parents died after I was born. Why? How did you know of her?"

"I'm so sorry to hear that. She was my daughter."

Sophie was taken aback with equal shock to what Jim was experiencing. "You're Jim's grandfather?"

Jenkins moved closer to Jim and placed his right arm on his shoulder. "Yes, Jim. I am your grandfather and I am in a very direct way the reason why you ended up here."

This was becoming a bit too much for Jim. First, he learned that Jenkins was related to him and now he believed that his so-called grandfather was beginning to speak in riddles probably, from old age and being confined too long by the Nartanian.

"Listen, we need to get out of here fast!" he said, only Jenkins became infuriated at him for dismissing him.

"Listen to what I have to say first, will you?"

"What, damnit?"

"Listen, Jim!" Sophie urged him.

"Right, go ahead!"

"I'm going to tell you how I ended up here.

The reason to why you were born with such rare and extremely great talent to discover the means in which to traverse the multiverse like you have been doing is because I made a pact with beings mostly made up of energy, consciousness, if you will, to "gift" my descendants and lineage with the capability of precognition."

Jim was astonished. "That's how I can remember the future?"

Jenkins smiled. "Yes but you are really remembering the past events of your previous life. You see time is a circle and when it is complete, it begins over again in the exact same fashion."

"Do you know how I can change this cycle?"

"No but the sentient entities may know how."

"Where did you meet these 'sentient entities'," asked Sophie.

"Maybe I'll tell you both that answer someday but we got to get out of here now," replied Jenkins.

Jim was unsure whether or not to believe him.

"Wait! you mean, everything I am is because of
these beings?"

"No. Just your gift. The rest was down to you and how you utilized that knowledge you gain from your gift."

Jim was now beginning to realize how his knowledge over the years presented itself as thought or mental impulses more like a sure instinct that was never based on mere feelings, as if he automatically knew stuff and always had the knowledge without questioning himself. He felt privileged and cheated.

"Why did you do this to me? Condemn me to fate without my consent. I could have been someone else."

Jenkins felt remorseful now. "I'm sorry, Jim. I had to do this because of my pact with these beings in which I would someday help them 'till I ended up being imprisoned here."

"Help them how?"

"When I first came here to this reality – when anyone goes into one reality from another – there is an upset in the subatomic structure of the reality they're visiting--"

"I know the virus. It is causing molecular melding, I think."

Sophie wasn't interested in listening to the two of them talk science. She was becoming irritated and her interest was in what Jenkins was telling them before Jim went on an adrenalin rush about the damned virus.

"Who lost out in this pact – let me guess, the Nartanian in this reality," Sophie said.

"No, the Nartanian weren't involved in the pact. They have other issues that I'm not aware of. They think I know something or that I'm hiding valuable information."

"What do you mean?" asked Jim and Sophie together.

"Look all, I know is that these beings of consciousness - sentient entities if you will - they are two mates and one of them is sick, the equivalent of being mentally unstable; her consciousness is emanating her disturbed thoughts in the form of shockwaves. The virus that you have already encountered is acting like a conduit for these shockwaves and if you don't find a cure for it, the sick sentient entity will infect everybody no matter what reality they reside in with infernal telepathic images leading to chaos as well as the physical melding of all living matter."

"Just when I thought my job was a freedom fighter now I have to cure a quantum virus I thought I caused. But if I remember right the virus doesn't adhere to any physical laws that I'm aware of," replied Jim.

"No, and if we don't help her – it, she, will consume the multiverse!"

Sophie was thinking hard about what Jenkins had just told Jim.

"Wait, did you say 'beings'?"

"Yes, more like a consciousness."

"That's it!" Sophie said. "That's who was trying to communicate to me when the virus was surrounding me. – they're evil!"

She then turned to Jenkins and pushed him up against the wall. "You are evil, Jenkins! Jim, you can't trust him!"

Jim pulled her away from his grandfather.

"What's the matter with you, Sophie? Feisty like someone else that I once knew!"

"You don't get it! What went through my head when I was infected by the virus – it was horrendous!" Sophie screamed.

Jenkins placed his hands on her head. She calmed down.

"My dear, it's not evil. This being is sick, and I'm sorry you had to experience this first hand. We need to get out of here so I can make right this wrong situation that I have caused."

Sophie nodded her head, sobbing. Jim watched her tears as they fell from her eyes and realized there was humanity to this girl even though she concealed it all too well.

CHAPTER TWENTY TWO

The leader of what Jim and Sophie termed the bad Nartanian was a humanoid alien being and, like all of his race, he had a svelte, rangy figure with light blue skin. Both Jim and Sophie hadn't encountered any Nartanian directly because there was only a small number on their planetoid and they were generally xenophobic by nature. They did not trust humans. Xon Prime was the ruler of all Nartanian for most of his adult life where their life span was three times that of the average life span of human beings. He was bitter at the loss of his home planet when it one day migrated to Hudson's reality leaving him and most of his people behind to fend for themselves without a home, not to mention Jenkins's deal with the energy beings to seize Xon's people's minds to appease the ailing consciousness being. The taste of vengeance on his tongue was becoming increasingly washed with a deluge of delectable delight and he wanted Jenkins - and all humanity across the multiverse - to be eradicated for stealing his homeworld.

Xon had just reviewed the report from the human guard that captured Jim and Sophie, a human which he had enslaved to become obsequies to his every request. Most of the other humans on this Earth were enslaved to service Xon. This human was Sam Crawford, yes, the parallel version of Sears's right-hand man.

Crawford took off his mask and bowed before Xon. "My lord, shall I undergo preparations to have them executed?"

"No!!! You inept, pitiful human, I want their DNA and subatomic structures analyzed. I want to determine which reality they originated from – then I want to locate it."

"My lord. The young man exclaimed he knew Al Hudson. Does that name sound familiar to you?"

"What?! Bring him here to me at once!"

"Yes, my lord."

Crawford gestured to his guards to get Jim.

Jim was thrown on the hard rock ground in front of Xon. He screeched with agony and was perplexed at seeing for the first time an extraterrestrial being.

"Miserable human, state your name."

Jim swallowed the lump in his throat. His left arm was aching, probably fractured. He winced and managed to utter his name.

"Speak up!" Xon yelled.

"Jim Callaghan."

"You claim to know of the whereabouts of Al Hudson. Tell me how to get to his reality, or I can assure you that your friends will suffer an excruciating death."

"No!!! Please! Leave them alone. Okay, you should be able to determine the route back to Hudson's reality via the device you took from me when we got here."

Jim was referring to the QBE which Crawford took from him.

"What device?" asked Xon.

"The one the masked human took from me."

Xon began to experience rage through his veins as if it were molten lava running through them. The parallel Crawford who was in the other room and who was listening hurried into Xon's chamber.

"Crawford?!" Jim said and was now astonished and a little confused but soon realized he must be an alternative version of him.

Xon observed, "You know this pitiful human, Jim?"

"I know that you can't trust him."

Crawford knew he had screwed up. "Wait, my lord – I can explain!"

"Where is that device?"

"He's lying. There was no device with him. Please my lord! Haven't I always proven my loyalty to you?"

Xon simpered a smile, and then his smile

broke into an expression that was sadistic. He then pulled out a long syringe type of needle from his hip and gestured to Crawford to come closer to him. Crawford walked fretfully toward Xon, tears secreted by his dead eyes. Xon raised the needle and impaled Crawford's forehead, sticking it in through his brain. Crawford writhed with the discomfort and fell to the ground where he began to wriggle like someone in electric shock. He then evaporated.

Xon turned to Jim. "That is the cost of disobedience."

Jim flinched, and an icy chill almost paralyzed his spine. His thinking began to digress somewhat from his quest for justice for Sophie through vengeance; however he believed killing Sears when the time came would be less sadistic, thus justifying his goals.

"My apologies, Jim, for my extravagant methods. I tend to forget human beings are squeamish creatures."

"I guess it had to be done," replied Jim.

"Yes, indeed."

Jim now knew he had developed a rapport with Xon and decided to make a request. "Xon, I must say again the human female and I am innocent of your feud with Hudson. I beg of you to let us go."

"I will let you go but first I command you to use the QBE as you called it to locate Hudson and my planet, my home."

"If we do that, will you allow the old man to come with us?"

"Take him, he's nothing but a tiresome nuisance anyway."

"You've got a deal, Xon."

One day passed and in that time, Xon allowed Jim, Sophie and Jenkins to get cleaned up, provided them with new clothes and treated them to some decent food. They were just finishing dessert when one of Xon's staff summoned all three of them to meet with him in his courtyard. Jim, with the Nartanian's scientists help, adjusted the QBE to relocate Hudson's reality. However, Jim was baffled somewhat. He understood the sophistication of their technology, especially when Hudson used it to cure the virus previously - however, he couldn't figure out how they corrected the QBE's relocation determining software which was designed to retrace the coordinates of the alternative realities visited by them. There was also something else that was perplexing to Jim, a modification to the device itself.

They waited for Xon quite nervously and Sophie and Jenkins noticed how preoccupied Jim was with his modified QBE which Xon's servant just gave him before they entered the courtyard. Sophie tried to break the ice, trying to add some sense of normality to the situation. "So Mister Jenkins, you've been absent from your home for a long time. What's the first thing that you're going to do after we get home?"

Jenkins didn't answer her. He wasn't listening to her. Instead, he was intently watching his grandson. "Jim, you must not trust this alien. He imprisoned me for decades, tortured me and starved me. He is only using you for his own gain."

Jim sighed - a sigh that did not feature acknowledgment at what his grandfather just said but of slight contempt.

"What do you expect me to do? Huh? I have to make a deal with a devil to topple and bring to justice another devil! I can't be expected to keep my hands clean. Anyway, Hudson lied to us. He robbed these aliens of their technology and allowed them to die. I thought creative expression being prohibited by Sears was grounds to stand up and fight, then my Sophie's callous murder and now genocide – I won't rest 'till all of these bad guys are put in their place!"

Jenkins took in a deep breath and went to lie down. Sophie was impressed. "Just how did your Sophie 'betray you'?"

"Not now. I'm trying to think,"replied Jim.

"Well too bad. One minute you can't take your eyes off me and the rest of the time I feel hate vibes emanating from you toward me. What did she do?"

"I'll tell you what she did!"Jim replied angrily. "We were together Planing a partnership and as soon as I sent her on her first assignment for the

Underground she gets herself killed and I don't even know if she slept with that Crawford or not. The worst thing about the whole thing is that *I* sent her on that assignment – I gave her away and we were never really together in the way it mattered!"

"Sounds so similar to my reality in the form that I may not be too dissimilar to your Sophie."

"What do you mean?"

"If she had a mother like mine and a very ill father then she would be forced to do anything for them to stay alive."

"Yeah, come to think of it my Sophie had a very similar background."

"You see, don't be too hard on her memory and stop punishing me for sending her to Crawford in the first place!"

"Since when did I 'punish' you?"

"Ever since you and Richard landed in my reality. I could see it in your eyes."

"I apologize. It's not easy to have a living reminder of a memory that I keep tarnishing with my anger. It wasn't really her fault – any of it. It was mine. I shouldn't have sent her on that assignment and I guess I am a product of a repressive environment like Apollo City. All I know is anger. I'm truly sorry, Sophie."

Jim pondered for a moment and reflected with a deep introspective thinking. He realized he had been indeed hard on his Sophie's memory because of his selfish male pride and decided there and then not to take it out on the alternate Sophie anymore. After all it was his demons that he would have to make peace with later on when he got things sorted.

CHAPTER TWENTY THREE

J im, Sophie and Jenkins were standing outside Xon's palace. It seemed alien in its appearance and its structure was triangular. The gardens surrounding it consisted of Earth and Nartanian hybrid plants. He had tried to grow intrinsically Nartanian vegetation, but this resulted in failure. Xon resented in eating human plants as he saw it as degrading and another reason to avenge his world but most of all he hated the fact that Hudson must be laughing at night knowing that.

Jim gazed around his surroundings. Yet again he felt a little queasy breathing natural air and being in natural surroundings after spending all his life confined to an artificial biosphere on the moon. Sophie, unlike her original counterpart from Jim and Jenkins's version of Apollo City, was aloof and much too preoccupied to notice the difference. She had one goal – bloodthirsty revenge. She was still of the mindset that Jim was always the same man she always knew and not from another distinct reality to hers. It didn't make any difference to her whom her perceived enemies were. They were her enemies no matter what difference in their particle make up. Jenkins's goal was singular compared to Sophie and Jim's. He wanted to put right what he did wrong decades earlier and that was to help the ailing condition of this being of consciousness.

The three of them were soon snapped out of their individual reverie when they heard strident sounding walking coming towards them. They could not recognize who was approaching them. They were four individuals marching and they had a kind of metallic armor covering their bodies. One of them went over to Jim. The armor surrounding its head vanished revealing Xon himself.

Jim opened up his eyes figuratively speaking and saw how advanced Nartanian technology really was.

"Xon, was that metal or just an energy field camouflaging your head just there?"

Xon laughed and was irritated somewhat at the simplicity of Jim's marvel, reminding himself of the fact that these simple humans - or alternative versions of them - stole his world and allowed his people to perish. Jim knew he had put his foot in it and changed the subject.

"Have you got my QBE?"

Xon took the device out of his armor. "It's

ready and we will not waste any more time."

He gave the device back to Jim and to him it felt like a child finding a long lost toy.

"Are you all ready?" he asked.

They nodded their heads. Jim pointed the QBE's head toward empty space and activated it. The swirling vortex reappeared and they each casually entered it, followed by Xon and two of his soldiers.

It was raining on Hudson's earth. The vortex emerged and Jim, Sophie, Jenkins and Xon exited from it. There was no sign of Xon's two soldiers.

Xon was shaken up a little and tried to regain his tough composure quickly before the others noticed.

Jim was feeling glad to be back somewhere familiar. "That was the smoothest ride I ever had through the vortex!"

Sophie winced. "When do we get down to do it?" She looked around. "Where are your soldiers?"

Xon simpered a smile.

"They were just holograms. I have everything that I require here."

"What do you mean?" asked Jenkins.

Xon didn't answer him. Instead he turned his back and began heading toward Hudson's parliament.

"Where are we going and how are we supposed to defeat an entire army?"

Xon turned to Jim.

"I think I should refine that little device of yours. I felt shaken in transit."

Jim handed him the QBE. Xon grabbed it and began flicking it in an anticlockwise motion twice then very quickly back clockwise.

"There, that should make the journey smoother as you say for next time."

Two of Hudson's guards suddenly took them by surprise.

"Halt, you are not from here! Who are you?"

Xon approached the guards and they raised their rifles.

"I am here to see First Prelate Al Hudson. Tell him Xon is back."

"What's he doing? Is he nuts?" Jenkins asked Sophie.

"I don't know – there's something fishy about this entire situation," she replied.

One of the guards took out his com transceiver and told his superior the situation. He then moved carefully over to Xon.

"Come with us now, all of you!"

Jim signaled to Sophie and Jenkins to follow Xon along with himself. Sophie was skeptical.

"Jim, why are you blindly following Xon? He's only out for himself."

"What choice do I have? It's a means to an end. An end that I hope will be pretty soon."

"Quiet! No talk amongst you!" yelled the other guard.

As they followed the guards, more guards

converged around them escorting them to the same building where Jim first met Hudson and treated him as a guest.

What nobody saw was a slight bubbling of a gelatinous substance that was multiplying at an exponential rate just where Xon and Jim were standing moments earlier.

They were all brought before Hudson. He came to the barracks where Xon, Jim, Sophie and Jenkins were in custody. He did not appear the welcoming benefactor Jim first met weeks earlier - instead he seemed irate and fearsome.

"What is the meaning of this, Xon? Do you really believe that you can harm me here right on my own doorstep?"

"I already have," Xon replied, then laughed sadistically.

Hudson turned to Jim and struck him.

"I gave you the means to help you and your people to cure the virus and yet you ally yourself with this barbarian!"

Jim rubbed his cheek. Hudson's guards poised themselves in case he tried anything.

"Xon told me you cheated him and allowed his race to perish. Is that true?"

"I did what I had to do and now I have to stoop to his level once again. Guards, take them into the execution chamber immediately!"

Just then one of Hudson's other guards rushed into the barracks.

"The first Prelate, that virus we fixed a few

weeks ago is back!"

"Just neutralize it like before!"

Xon laughed aloud.

"You see, I modified it. It will consume this entire quantum universe in no time at all and I and my friends are immune."

Hudson knew he couldn't stop it and as he tried to think, his mind was flooded with barbaric images of the Nartanian he allowed to die, but these images were not his memories – instead, these were coming from the ill Sentient Entities amplifying them. As he tried to move away he was enveloped by the gelatinous distorting matter that was now everywhere.

Jenkins grabbed Xon. "What have you done? You're no better than he ever was now!"

Those words began to reverberate through Jim's mind like echoes and he quickly shut down his thinking just enough for his survival instinct to alert him to get out of there fast.

Sophie saw how Jim was easily becoming distracted and yelled, "Jim, reactivate the QBE now!"

Jim, against his better judgment, signaled to Xon. He shook his head. Jim pushed the main button on the device and Sophie, Jenkins and finally himself entered its mouth.

CHAPTER TWENTY FOUR

As Xon witnessed Jim, Sophie and Jenkins leaving the diseased universe, he was about to give up when a female Nartanian gestured over to him to join her. He found her incredibly attractive and couldn't resist her beauty. She placed her arms around him and vanished from this infected reality just as Jim and the others had moments earlier.

Back on the original Apollo City, Sears was in his office studying more effective and brutal ways of eliminating the Underground once and for all. He began to feel a shiver streak down his spine and someone calling out in an enchanted voice. She was crying out, "Edmund" repeatedly. He was scared like a little child hearing ghost stories for the first time.

He stood up from his specially designed leather chair and yelled out, "What do you want from me?"

An old woman appeared before him. She gave off an air of feebleness and fragility.

"Edmund, after all I done for you."

"You?"

"Yes, me. And I have brought someone here with me."

She pointed to the corner of his office and Xon

emerged out of thin air.

"What's that?"

"What matters is you're in danger and I have to modify our arrangement."

"For you, yes, but for me – look at me – I'm dying!"

"What do you want me to do? I'll do anything to help you as I'm in your eternal gratitude."

She turned to Xon. He became conscious.

"Xon," she said. "This here is a human you can trust. His name is Sears. I want you to share everything you know about the virus. Understood?"

"Why, yes. I owe you for saving my life just moments ago."

With that, she vanished. Xon looked around him and scanned Sears' office with his eyes. He noticed a neuro-resequencer on the desk.

"That's what I used to change the virus. I got it off a human –"

"It's just a common brain chemistry suppressor device," interrupted Sears. "I will use the AI systems combined with our knowledge to devise a means of controlling the virus."

Sears moved over to his desk and gestured to Xon to shove it over to one side. There was a compartment door located on the floor. Sears opened up his tunic and pulled out a chain with a key attached to it. He pulled the key off the chain and opened the compartment with it. There - to Xon's astonishment - was a pulsating crystal.

"This crystal was given to me four decades ago by the woman creature that you just saw. I need your expertise on how to harness it to yield its full potential."

"Yes. I can apply the same methods I did to that

suppressor device," replied Xon.

Sears locked the door to his office and they both spent a number of hours using the AI system to control the crystal.

Sears marveled at the finished product.

"You see, Mister Xon, the waves emanating from this crystal can correct the virus. The virus is something I first became aware of a long time ago when I had much bigger ambitions. Now I have to make do with just one reality. Or do I?"

Xon became nervous. His warrior instincts were letting him know that this human was just as barbaric as himself and couldn't be trusted.

"Sounds like to me, Sears, that you've got all this figured out."

Sears laughed. "Oh, yes I have. You see, I waited a long time for someone to come into this reality from another. I couldn't do it myself because the risks were too high. She gave you me as a gift and your body contains the virus so that the crystal could read its frequency range."

Xon realized quickly what was going on here.

"You treacherous human. I should've known not to trust you!"

Xon was about to charge into Sears when Sears pulled out a gun and fired on him. Xon fell to the ground. Sears went over to him.

"You see, your death is not in vain."

Xon tried desperately to keep alive and as the laser impact still burned through his alien flesh he became even more resilient. The frail woman reappeared and she moved over to Sears.

"You almost killed him. Good job you didn't. You need from him the frequency in which the reaction takes place between positive energy and negative energy. Once you have it, you will become unstoppable."

Sears was wearing a big grin on his fat face. "I'll use this."

He picked up a neuro-resequencer and applied the beam to the Nartanian's head. Xon struggled. The frail woman placed her hands over his head.

"Such hatred in this being's mind. I should've used him instead of you all those years ago."

"Glad you didn't," replied Sears.

"I have it!" she screamed.

She grabbed Sears by the shoulder and pressed her hands on his head. Sears was obviously experiencing discomfort and then smiled.

"Sears, I have used most of my energy in calling to this reality and bringing him here. When you are ready, you must summon me at our original meeting place, understood?"

"I understand."

She moved over to Xon. He was now dead and they both vanished. Sears was pleased. He accessed the computer on his desk and inputted quantum calculations. He lifted up the crystal and began staring at it. It started pulsating in different colors as he touched it and it became smaller and smaller as if he was absorbing it. He heard the chime on his door sound followed by Crawford's voice. He yelled, "Do not disturb me again!"

Crawford apologized and left. Sears stood upright and raised his hands. He looked peculiar and began phasing in and out of the space/time continuum. He spoke grandiosely, "Now I have unlimited power. Nobody can halt my dominance over the multiverse."

CHAPTER TWENTY FIVE

Back on the original Apollo City biosphere, life hadn't changed that much except for Sears's crackdown on the remaining Underground members. One of these was Richard. The moment he returned back to the biosphere he was captured and imprisoned. He was tortured and it was becoming more brutal by the day. Sears wanted to know the whereabouts of Jim Callaghan and believed Richard was hiding him. The day before, Richard was subjected to electrodes implanted on sensitive areas of his body and today was the day where the current was going to be increased to maximum, enough to cause excruciating pain but not death. Sam Crawford oversaw Richard's interrogation and painstakingly selected each means to make him more cooperative.

Crawford always had an impeccable record of professionalism and diligence and was extremely tenacious in his methods. He could barely come to terms with the blemish on his present record – the unexplained disappearance of the so-called Underground leader Jim Callaghan.

Crawford entered the interrogation room. Richard was strapped to a bed of steel and connected to wires and electrodes. There was a voltage regulator along with a crude life signs detector just a few feet from the bed. The room was stony grey in color and devoid of any décor - not even the municipal police emblem was anywhere to be seen. It was also quite cold.

Richard was dreading what was about to come his way. He had a fairly average pain threshold but the fear of pain of this degree was too much. Tears ran down his cheeks. He cried out in his mind for Jim to come back and free him and everyone else on Apollo City. He heard Crawford shouting. He was shouting at one of the municipal police officers. Richard opened and reopened his eyes in quick succession to dry his tears when he saw: Abigail sitting beside him. He tried to speak but she uttered, "Shush!"
Crawford ran into the interrogation room and saw Abigail.

"Abigail, your wife? I had her put to death!"

"That's right! You had me put to death too," said Sophie Ramirez – the one who belonged to this Apollo City.

"What's going on here?" Crawford asked, nearly white with shock.

Both Abigail and Sophie turned into bizarre

looking creatures and began to roar. Then they vanished as if there were never there.

A cold sweat ran down Richard's almost naked prone body. "You see them too. I told you it's the quantum virus! Now, do you believe me?"

Crawford was still skeptical and being a consummate suspicious military leader he didn't except this.

"Our great Governor outlawed that kind of science for decades and you're telling me some dilettante like Jim Callaghan invented a magic device to allow him to visit other realities – there's only one reality, one universe – this universe! And I won't tolerate your heresy any longer!"

He switched on the voltage regulator and set it to the maximum.

Richard screamed until he was out cold. Sears barged inside the room and yelled to Crawford, "Sam, turn that off. We need him alive to cooperate!"

Crawford turned the regulator off and while Richard was still unconscious, Sears turned to him.

"This has all got to do with Thomas Jenkins."

"Jenkins died before you took over the biosphere. What do you mean, Governor?"

"I don't believe he's dead. Somehow he can help us all now. You were in no doubt a witness to the shared hallucinations that everybody is experiencing?"

"Yeah, I thought I saw his dead wife and Sophie Ramirez, then they turned into grotesque animals."

Sears took a moment. "Hum, I haven't been always fully honest with you. There is a being who lives outside of this universe that is causing this mayhem. That's one of the reasons why I had such strict policies on science and art. I feared somehow it would lead to communication with this being or spirit. That's why I banished Jenkins from here."

"You mean to tell me that Richard here is telling the truth?"

"Yes, Sam. He is."
Crawford felt betrayed at the lack of trust that Sears obviously failed to have in him since he began his reign.

"I can understand, Sam, why you wouldn't trust me now or even believe any of this but I require your loyalty and obedience now more than ever. You see Callaghan and possibly Jenkins will be back here any day now. I'm offering you this biosphere in exchange for your help in defeating them all."

Crawford was taken aback. He couldn't believe his ears. Up until this, he was going to have Sears himself lying on the bed filled with the electrodes so he could torture him into giving him the password for the mainframe.

"Are you telling me that you are going to retire when all of this is resolved?"

"That's precisely what I'm saying."

"And I get your job?"

"Yes."

"What do I have to do?"

"First of all, upon the return of Callaghan and his motley crew, arrange to have them executed. Second, you and I are going to take a little trip outside the biosphere to the Darker. That's where there's a small, no longer used station where we can make contact with the Sentient Entities."

"You know all of this, how?"

"Unbeknownst to Jenkins, I dealt with her before."

Crawford wasn't sure anymore who or what to believe. He thought he was head of security and most of his adult life that's what he was but now he was beginning to deal with elements of metaphysics and - from his point of view - even the supernatural.

"Sam, come on! We don't have much time!"

"Yes, Governor. What do we do with him?"

"Barker, just imprison him. While you were too busy torturing him, one of your subordinates noticed he had been experimenting on something. When we come back I want to find out what. I want no loose ends. This time I'm going to wrap up things right – so I can retire in comfort."

At a restricted location near the outer rim in the Municipal Sector, there was a shuttle launch pad equipped with two remaining working shuttlecrafts. This area was under high security and was virtually unknown to most of Apollo City's residents. Crawford himself only ever heard references to it throughout his career and never decided to investigate it.

The automated security server allowed Sears and Crawford inside the docking area. Its appearance was old as the original fit of the biosphere before the administration modernized it. It was also quite dusty and unkempt throughout. Sears signaled Crawford to follow him and stop gawking. They went over to the shuttle crafts which were small but big enough to carry four people each.

"Which one should we take?" Sears asked Crawford.

"How should I know? Can we trust either of them?"

Sears grinned. "You're not getting cold feet on me now, Sam?"

"Of course not. I was never outside of the biosphere, that's all. I don't want to be stranded on some remote outpost in the middle of the Darker."

"Now is not the time to cease your trust in me. I believe I know what I'm doing. Trust me, will you, Sam?"

"Always, sir."

Sears took out a key card and slid it through the card reader. Nothing happened. He looked at the card and then the reader and noticed there was dust on them. He took a deep breath and blew into the reader's card slot and wiped the card against his tunic. He then tried again and this time the shuttle lit up and its door opened.

Crawford was not used to solving such problems with this kind of simplicity. He was more into taking drastic actions as his job demanded at times and watched in awe but quickly snapped himself out of it in case Sears would correct him again. He looked carefully inside the shuttle as if he was making a gamble on it being okay. He noticed the interior was pristine, like it was in the condition that it came off the assembly line in. The seating appeared to be comfortable and gave him the impression that their journey to the Darker would be smooth and seamless.

"Don't spend the rest of the day admiring the view, Sam – hop inside," Sears said.

Crawford quickly jumped inside the shuttle. When Sears told you to do something, you did it. Sears followed him inside and pulled out the control pad that sounded like a lever coming out. He then pushed a button and the door shut closed.

Sears continued to input commands into the control pad. The launch pad door that was large enough to accommodate both shuttles opened. The shuttle steadily exited the biosphere. Crawford watched the deep black of space as they were both immersed into it. He gazed at the ailing Earth and thought, how did all this ever happen? The shuttle made its trajectory to the dark side of the moon for what would be a short journey.

CHAPTER TWENTY SIX

The portal reappeared back in Jim's apartment. Jim, Sophie and Jenkins stepped out of it without any friction. Sophie was somewhat jilted by the journey from Hudson's now crumbling reality. Jenkins turned to Jim and asked, "Am I finally home, son?"

"Yes, Granddad, you are."

Sophie looked around at the architecture.

"My God, it's virtually identical to my Apollo City!"

"I guess the ride there wasn't as smooth for you as Granddad and me?"

"No, it was rough."

"That's because we're from here. I must find Richard. We've got to finally deal with Sears and Crawford."

Jim went into his bedroom to find his makeshift computer to notice it had been confiscated by the administration. "Damn! They took everything!"

"I presume they want to take control over the mainframe – well I know the back door key!" said Jenkins.

"Let's do this right away. There's no more time to lose."

They crept out of Jim's apartment to find it wasn't necessary. Security must have been out on a refreshment break it seemed as the residential sector was no longer in lockdown. Jim found this odd. He was sure security would be tight, especially after his and Richard's sudden disappearance weeks ago. He turned to Jenkins and asked, "Do you know something I don't know?"

Jenkins frowned. "As a matter of a fact I'm suspecting Sears has gone to the Darker."

"Why? What the hell is out there?"

"I'll tell you, son. There was a remote outpost I built. I designed it to communicate with Earth. I thought he knew nothing about it but he must have found out after he banished me."

"You still haven't answered Jim's question," demanded Sophie.

"Okay, okay – you remember not so long ago I said I would answer your questions about how I first discovered the Sentient Entities?"

"Plainly," replied Sophie.

"Well, Sophie and Jim, it was there in the Darker. I was there shortly after it was constructed when I felt their presence. At first, I thought I was losing my mind. Then it became clear that they were another form of life. I communicated with them for hours on end. Then they revealed to me that Earth would experience a massive catastrophe and that I could help to prevent this. They spoke in riddles, and I couldn't make them out at the best of times. Then the asteroid bombardment occurred and it was too late. When I returned to the outpost from the biosphere they were gone, and on my way back to Apollo City I was arrested, and it dawned on me that a coup-de-tat had taken place there. Sears exiled me. One thing though, these sentient entities promised me that my theories would be given a prop up and also my lineage would have my knowledge like personality traits."

"You already told me all of this. Well, at least my so-called 'gift' part of it anyway. Just why would Sears be going there?" Then it dawned on Jim. "He knows the Sentient Entities too!"

Jenkins found his grandson's logic much too incredulous. "How could he? He doesn't believe in any of this!"

Jim perceived his grandfather's tone of voice to be condescending.

"He must have some reason to have gone there. Can we follow him somehow?"

"Now you're beginning to make sense, son. I know where the docking pad is located and if we're lucky there should be another shuttle available there. assuming Sears hasn't destroyed it already," said Jenkins, grinning at his self believed cunningness.

"Right, we will leave the mainframe for now

and head for this docking bay, wherever it is."

As they made their way to the docking bay, they discovered that their fellow citizens were oblivious to recent events. When they got there they noticed the entrance to the docking bay was still open due to Sears's haste in heading for the Darker. Jim and Sophie were in childlike awe, especially Jim at the mere existence of the facility. He thought if only he had known of its existence sooner he could have exiled Sears on Mars or something.

Jenkins wasn't thinking or contemplating what ifs. He was much too busy checking out the remaining shuttle.

"It's big enough to fit four. Is your friend Richard coming?"

"No. Richard is convalescing. Crawford's torture really took a lot out of him," replied Jim.

"Just as well. We need to go now. Hop in!" Jenkins replied and urged Jim and Sophie to hurry up.

They jumped inside quickly and the shuttle's door closed. Sophie wondered how Jenkins was going to get this thing moving. He tapped in a code and everything went dead until a few moments later it became alive again with a whining sound and lit up all over.

"We're good to go," he said.

The shuttle ejected the biosphere on a trajectory to the remote outpost in the Darker. Jim almost grew fatigued at the grey stone surface and the pitch black of space. Luckily these shuttles could fly at high speeds. He rubbed his eyes, sighed and made a wish that all of this calamity would soon end. He closed his eyes and paused for thought for a second. He thought about his childhood and how repressive it was and how his parents pulled him through it with their occasional words of encouragement. When he reopened his eyes he was startled to see a tall triangular shaped structure that appeared to be made of marble staring him in the face. This was some kind of antenna.

"We're here," Jenkins said softly and a little bit nervously.

"Wow! Sophie exclaimed.

At the base of the structure was a rectangular building. Jenkins pointed out Sears's shuttle to Jim and Sophie, located at the opposite side of the structure.

Jenkins looked around the interior of the shuttle and tried to remember something. He went over to a hatch and pulled it open. There were four spacesuits left inside the compartment and he handed the others one each. They slipped into them and he regulated their oxygen as well as his own and finally switched on their helmets com systems to enable them to communicate with each other.

"Are you both ready?" he asked Jim and Sophie.

They nodded.

He opened the shuttle door and they tried to maneuver themselves with great difficulty to the entrance of the outpost.

After a lot of tumbling and swaying, they finally arrived at the outpost's entrance. Jenkins gestured to Jim to help him push it in. Sophie followed them inside.

The inside room was filled with computers, desks and seats. Sears and Crawford were waiting for them and the Sentient Entity.

"About time, Jenkins. Long-time no see," Sears said mocking him.

"You haven't changed a bit, Sears."

"Well, we will cut the small talk and unpleasantries. Just make that important call and summon up that being."

"There are two of them. How'd you know about any of this anyway?"

"I kept close eyes on you all those years ago."

"I see. One thing that escapes me though, why do you wish to speak to the Sentient Entities? They don't even know you."

"Oh yes, they do. As I said I had you monitored. I knew everything you did and everywhere you went, including here. I communicated with them before and I am going to do so now."

"Wait, what? Why?"

"Who do you think organized that little asteroid party decades back?"

"That was you? Billions died and perished!"

"It was all down to my master plan and you have to be ruthless to rule a paradise like my Apollo City."

"You genocidal maniac!"

Sophie took out a knife and headed toward Sears. Crawford intervened by stepping in front of him.

"No, Sophie! Don't!" yelled Jim.

"Why? He murdered billions, murdered the version of me from this reality and my friend, my version of you, Jim. Why wouldn't I?"

"He's nothing. Killing him would set a dangerous precedent for the new Apollo City in which we intend to lead. Don't stoop to his level, Sophie," replied Jim.

Sophie growled to herself and handed the knife over to Jim.

"You'd better be right."

Sears began to laugh sadistically at Jim.

"Way to go, Callaghan. I knew you hadn't the backbone to even punish me."

"Sears, why did you have to make restrictions on art and science? All it achieved was a stagnant society giving rise to rebellion. Or maybe you're sadistic enough to have a section of the population having nothing because it made you feel better, so you could feel like the big man?" Jim asked him.

"Art, science, all of which impedes technological progress. I didn't want a bohemian kind of society! I wanted to build a productive culture on Apollo City for people like me, not like the way it was on Old Earth – I'll never let that happen!"

Sophie laughed with a strong tone of sarcasm.

"I bet you were a nobody on Old Earth!"

Sears didn't answer her and give her a hateful look. Suddenly there was a build-up of energy like they never had seen. Two human figures morphed out from this energy.

Jim turned to Jenkins. "Are those them?"

"Yes, son. They are the Sentient Entities."

The strange beings of light and energy began to speak with angelic sounding voices. One of them wasn't making sense and speaking in riddles and sounded severely distressed.

The other began communicating: "It has been some time. My mate is ill. She is not going to survive much longer. I am frail also."

Jenkins, who was still feeling great anger at what these beings did to Old Earth, asked "Why did you make a deal with Sears? Both of you destroyed an entire civilization, the human race."

"It was her. She doesn't see the multiverse as I do. We are both very much different even though we are together."

Meanwhile Crawford, who had been fixated by Sophie and couldn't understand why she was alive again, moved over to her. Once beside her, he took out his gun and pointed it at her head.

"I thought I killed this bitch! What's she doing walking around like nothing's happened?"

Sears yelled at him, "Not now Crawford. Can't

you see we're busy?"

Crawford felt something sharp and cold pierce his back. He turned around and saw Jim with a bloody knife.

"You don't get to kill her a second time," Jim said.

Sears jumped over right beside Jim. "Now, Callaghan, you think you can murder my people who are you authority – your superiors?"

"He's not my superior. I do not answer to him, or you for that matter."

"Oh yeah? We will see about that!" Sears started swiping Jim. Jim tried desperately to block the onslaught.

Sophie clinched on to Jenkins. "Sears will kill him."

Jenkins yelled, "Use your precognition, Jim. Try to anticipate his next move."

Jim tried to do just that but failed. Sears was winning. Then came the final punch. Jim was dead. Sophie rushed over to his side. Jenkins looked at Sears.

"He was just a kid!"

The female Sentient Entity turned to Sears.

"Congratulations, you have beaten them all."

Those comments angered the male Sentient Entity. He grabbed her and began to drain the life from her. She screamed. Sears tried to help her but it was too late. She was gone. Jenkins moved closer to the energy being and implored him to stop Sears.

"I can do one better. I can intensify Jim's gift so he can be a match for Sears the next time around."

"He's dead! I killed him!" yelled Sears.

Jenkins picked up the bloody knife and stabbed Sears in the back, killing him.

The Male Sentient Entity continued. "Because I exist outside of the space/time continuum, I can enter it at any point. You will have to live your lives without your friend. However, in the next iteration of the causality cycle, Jim will have the power to use his talent in foreseeing the future. I am going to amplify his gift."

No sooner had this being spoken these words, he vanished. Jenkins and Sophie went back to the biosphere where they met Richard and told them everything. They changed Apollo City but something was amiss. They each lived out less than ordinary lives.

Time ended and the big bang happened all over, creating the same timeline as before right up to the point when Sears was about to kill Jim in the remote outpost in the Darker when Jim remembered Sears' next move as if he had lived through it before. He dodged it and drove into Sears, thrashing him. He kept on beating him. Sears was no match. Jenkins rushed over to him and punched Sears also.

"You are under arrest, Sears, for mass genocide and violation of human rights," he said as Sears was about to try to utter something.

"Speak up, Sears!" demanded Jim.

The male sentient entity intervened, "I saved you, however, I now no that I was in error. The point in time that is pivotal for your time line to change is the point when my mate made the bargain with Sears decades ago."

"What are you saying?" asked Jenkins.

"I am saying that I don't want this to happen again. None of it, the asteroid bombardment, Apollo City as Sears governed it, The original Sophie's death, I will make so that you have a second chance with her, Jim." He then vanished.

Jim picked up the knife and grabbed Sears but hesitated. "I can't do it."

Sophie grabbed the knife from his hand and finished Sears off. They left the Darker and reunited with Richard on the biosphere. Richard greeted Jim and the others, "Jim, remember your other self – James?"

Jim nodded.

"We have been working together and found a way to cure the virus using Xon's mutation principle to our advantage. We *can* cure the virus."

"That's really good. You know old friend, I strongly believe in another life time we will both have another chance of happiness for me with Sophie and for you, Abigail."

Richard paused to think for a second and smiled, "If you believe that then I will believe it too."

Deep down in Jim's heart he wondered if he would indeed get a second chance with the original Sophie and if sentient entities could in fact change things the next time around. In another lifetime he would find out. In the meantime he had to straighten Apollo City out and spent the remainder of his life jointly running the biosphere with his grandfather. The alternate Sophie married one of the former members of the Underground. Jim thought if things were different in another life if so to speak, he would remember everything that happened in this one and thus appreciate life more the next time around.

The End

Printed in Great Britain
by Amazon

27570842R00098